'I can outwit y
way, Justine,'
.ductively as he nibbled
e

'No ... I am not, positively not driving a one-armed bandit *anywhere*!'

He was still gripping her wrist, tightly, but his thumb caressed the back of her hand and that was far more painful. Tiny caresses that burned her skin.

'You are, dear Justine, because that is what I want——'

Dear Reader

This is the time of year when thoughts turn to sun, sand and the sea. This summer, Mills & Boon will bring you at least two of those elements in a duet of stories by popular authors Emma Darcy and Sandra Marton. Look out next month for our collection of two exciting, exotic and sensual desert romances, which bring Arab princes, lashings of sun and sand (and maybe even the odd oasis) right to your door!

The Editor

Natalie Fox was born and brought up in London and has a daughter, two sons and two grandchildren. Her husband, Ian, is a retired advertising executive, and they now live in a tiny Welsh village. Natalie is passionate about her cats, two strays brought back from Spain where she lived for five years, and equally passionate about gardening and writing romance. Natalie says she took up writing because she absolutely *hates* going out to work!

Recent titles by the same author:

LOVE OR NOTHING
POSSESSED BY LOVE
ONE MAN, ONE LOVE

THE FURY OF LOVE

BY

NATALIE FOX

MILLS & BOON

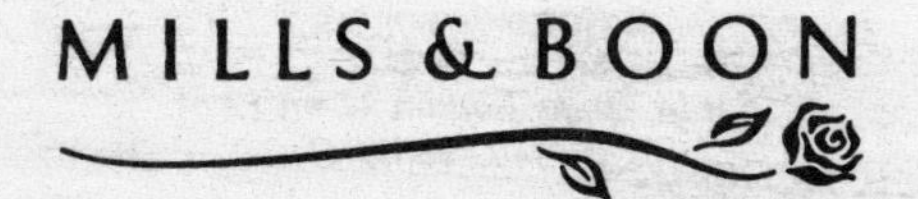

MILLS & BOON LIMITED
ETON HOUSE, 18-24 PARADISE ROAD
RICHMOND, SURREY TW9 1SR

All the characters in this book have no existence outside the imagination of the Author, and have no relation whatsoever to anyone bearing the same name or names. They are not even distantly inspired by any individual known or unknown to the Author, and all the incidents are pure invention.

First published in Great Britain 1994 by Mills & Boon Limited

This edition 1994

ISBN 0 263 78546 7

Set in Times Roman 11 on 12 pt.
01-9407-48891 C

Made and printed in Great Britain

CHAPTER ONE

'I DIDN'T like him then, I don't like him now and I won't like him tomorrow,' Justine stated unflinchingly, though her green eyes were ablaze with the backlash of what her sister had just told her—that Max Benedict was coming to dinner tonight and she would have to be nice to him, or else.

'How can you even suggest that I "be nice" to him tonight? If Daddy was hosting this dinner party——'

'Well, Daddy isn't, but my husband is,' Teresa declared forcefully. 'If you had been around lately you'd know the state the company was in and that Daddy is having to scour Europe for business and that Richard is struggling to get this contract from Max Benedict. This is what the dinner party is all about——'

'And this has nothing to do with me,' Justine fought back. 'If you want to ingratiate yourself into Daddy's favour by pulling this off while he's away, go ahead, but don't expect any help from me. I don't want anything to do with the family business, I never have, and Daddy knows that and accepts it.'

Determined green eyes warred back. Sisters at loggerheads again.

'Listen to me, Justine, because you are *not* in a position to argue. Black sheep of the family get tamed sooner or later and your time has come.'

So she was being tamed, was she? A punishment for her recalcitrance over the years? Yes, very probably, and the pity of it all was that Teresa was right, Justine thought miserably: she wasn't in a position to argue. Since coming back home after her business had failed she had been forced to eat humble pie for breakfast, lunch and dinner and now her sister, in her father's absence, was trying to force-feed her the loathsome Max Benedict. How could she 'be nice' to him when she disliked him so intensely?

'You came crawling back to the family home last month, broke and pitiful,' Teresa droned on, 'and it's about time you learned that Daddy isn't a charity——'

'I've never asked him for a penny,' Justine protested heatedly. She leaned forward to pour more tea as Teresa languished on the *chaise-longue* across from her in the drawing-room of their family home. Justine's hand was shaking at that unjust suggestion but she controlled it enough for her sister not to notice. So she had failed but she had never begged—and never would beg—money from their father.

'I came back because Daddy insisted,' she admitted, softly now because the heat had gone and she was remembering how her father was always there when she needed him in spite of the 'black sheep of the family' label her sister had saddled her with. She was well aware of how she had driven her father to distraction over the years and she was sorry for that now, but at least she had never begged money from him, not ever.

'And he insisted because he would have lost face if his youngest daughter had been found inhabiting a cardboard box under the arches at Waterloo.'

'Don't be so stupidly dramatic, Teresa. It wasn't that bad. I lost my business; so have thousands of others during this recession. I just need a breathing space to get myself together and Daddy understands that.'

'I doubt that,' Teresa bit scornfully. 'We never did understand you. You were always such a wilful child and nothing has changed since you've grown up, though Richard seems to think you never have—grown up, that is.'

Richard was her creepy brother-in-law who had certainly 'grown up' since marrying into the 'Hammond dynasty' as he liked to call it. He worked for John Hammond and had married his eldest daughter and his feet were well and truly under the table now. Well, if he was as smart as he thought he was he certainly didn't need Justine, the rebel, to 'be nice' to obnoxious mega-publishers like Max Benedict.

'I refuse to fawn on Benedict,' Justine told her sister firmly. 'It would be rude of me to refuse to dine with you but be it on your own heads how I behave. Remember the feeling is mutual. He dislikes me as much as I dislike him; in fact I'd go as far as to say you are putting Richard's career on the line by even putting Benedict and me in the same room—*and* there's a full moon tonight.'

Humour was lost on Teresa. Newly pregnant, she lay pale and wan on the *chaise-longue*, starting as she meant to go on, and it boded ill for the rest of the family. Teresa never had pulled much weight in the family business but because she had married a man who thought he did she felt exonerated from any further involvement in the set-up, apart from giving outlandish orders to Justine when she felt the need to exert her elder-sibling status. And now she was pregnant and going to produce the wonder of the age for the 'Hammond dynasty,' the *male* wonder of the age, of course, the grandson that John Hammond craved. This coming child was nothing to do with its father, apart from being conceived as a result of him, Justine thought cuttingly. Teresa was having this baby for *her* father, to prove to him that at least one of his daughters had worth.

Her sister eyed her narrowly. 'You really do despise the man, don't you?'

'Despise?' Justine rolled the word around her mouth. 'It doesn't go as deep as that. To despise someone shows an enormous depth of negative feeling which I don't feel for him. I don't hate, simply dislike, something quite different but enough. But...' she stated firmly, her eyes piercing into her sister's '...if you force me to be sweet to him tonight I could very well learn to despise him and him me and that would do Hammond Paper no good whatsoever. Instead of buying our paper for his publishing empire he could very well *not* and——'

'And that would be death to Hammond's, death to Daddy and——'

'And this is blackmail,' Justine breathed hopelessly, closing her eyes for a brief second, emotional blackmail and family politics rolling together and balling her into a corner. Was she really down to this, having to do something she didn't want to for the sake of her father, for the salvation of the family business? Oh, damn this recession—no one was free from it. Except a man like Max Benedict who was immune to every virus that stalked the earth. Giants like him weren't vulnerable...

Teresa tapped her empty plate for attention. 'Pass me one of those fondant delights, Justine. It's agony to stretch.'

Automatically she leaned forward to place a pale pink fondant on to her sister's plate, automatically because her mind was on that first meeting with Benedict when he had crushed her so completely.

She'd reached for the stars that night four years ago. She had been about to emerge from the cloying chrysalis of teenage youth into blossoming beauty, a beauty that all had said would take her far in life. The trouble was that at that age she had been blindingly naïve and totally lacking in modesty and actually believed she was beautiful. Cosmetically she supposed she had been with well spaced green eyes, tumbling Titian hair, full lips, a perfectly shaped face, and a figure that had escalated from scrawny youth to not so scrawny womanhood. Beauty went deeper than the reflection in a mirror, of course, but at the time Justine hadn't known that. She had thought her looks alone would have floored Benedict at the beastly magazine launch in Belgravia that her father had dragged her unwillingly along to. Yes, she had been a wilful handful at the time, not a very nice person to know, but then Max Benedict wasn't exactly Mr Personable himself.

'The arrogant creep,' she muttered reflectively under her breath, unfortunately loud enough for Teresa to pick up on.

'You really can be a bitch at times, Justine,' Teresa murmured softly, and then added with one of those lethal punches that always had a knack of winding Justine, 'But then if I'd been spurned by Benedict the beddable I'd be pretty miffed too.'

The colour started rising from her toes and in a second had engulfed her. Justine sat rigid, cheeks flaming, heart pulsing feverishly. She had forgotten that her sister had been witness to that humiliation, thank God the only witness.

'I wasn't spurned,' she admitted quickly, and then smiled to overcome the heated embarrassment that had her flesh creeping. 'Just overlooked, and Max Benedict is very accomplished at that.'

Overlooked? Hardly. He had looked all right; he couldn't have failed too after Justine in a mad moment of rebellion against the whole stuffy atmosphere of a boring old magazine launch stroke cocktail party had cornered him by the potted azaleas. His fascinating blue eyes, a striking feature set as they were against black hair and a devastating Côte d'Azur suntan, had looked her up and down and then straight through her as if she had just floated out of a magic lamp and wasn't really there at all. She hadn't even planned what to say to him, all she had known was that he was the most impressive man she had ever seen in her life and she just had to say *something* to him, to hold him there just long enough for him to fall madly in love with her and insist on sweeping her off into the sunset. Ah, the stuff of teenage hopes and dreams.

Reality had been humiliating, the way he had gripped her shoulders, moved her aside because she was in the way and mumbled under his breath, 'Not now, sweetheart,' as if she was a child begging for attention. Which she had been, of course.

'His standards are high, Justine, and you just didn't reach them,' Teresa added, dabbing at her mouth with a napkin.

'Thanks for the compliment,' Justine mumbled, reaching for the last fondant delight, desperately needing its sugary comfort.

Yes, she had reason to dislike him, he had hurt and humiliated her with his cold rejection at a tentative time of her life, but there was more, another reason for that mounting dislike, though no one needed know it—it was an even worse embarrassment to bear, one that even now made her cringe for her naïveté and childishness.

Justine moved then, drew herself away from the blazing fire in the drawing-room and went to the mullioned windows that overlooked the grounds of the Hammond estate in Berkshire. It was late November, mid-afternoon and almost dark already, but she could still see what was left of the estate. The stables and paddocks, the pine woods that had been just copses when she had played there as a child. Already her father had had to sell off some of his land to support the paper mill in Scotland. It would kill him if he had to sell the manor too.

She wrapped her arms around her and felt the chill of recession once again. The rebel had rebelled her last. She felt her individuality slipping away from her. She had tried so hard to break away and failed miserably and now her father and the family business needed Max Benedict's contract desperately, though what her sister thought she could achieve tonight at this wretched dinner party she couldn't begin to imagine.

'It won't work, you know,' Justine said as she moved back to the coffee-table to clear away the tea things. 'Being nice to Benedict won't get his contract. He doesn't work that way.' And Justine should know. Hadn't she tried herself, using her father's name to wheedle her way into his empire to try and sell her work to him? A second rejection, though that time she hadn't tried to impress him with her looks, just her talent, which he had equally sourly thrown back in her face.

'Justine, we have staff to do that,' Teresa remonstrated. 'That's the trouble with you; you're totally lacking in awareness of what's right and wrong. As a kid you drove poor Daddy mad by playing with the gardener's kids——'

'Cool it, Teresa. You know how I've always felt about the lord of the manor show you and Daddy always put on. If Mother were here now she'd be doing the very same thing herself——'

'How would you know? You can't even remember her!' Teresa snapped irritably.

Justine's fingers tightened around the tray as she lifted it from the table. True, she couldn't remember her, but she knew she was her mother's daughter, she felt it deep inside her. It was probably what had driven her mother into the arms of another man, this oppressive Hammond dynasty thing that crushed individual thinking. Her mother had been an artist, a wild spirit, a bohemian of her time. This life of servants and power struggles had suffocated her as it was suffocating Justine now. And John Hammond had recognised it in his younger daughter and railed against her so. God, she had never been able to do anything right for him as a child, nor now in adulthood. Teresa was fast becoming the new lady of the manor and loving it all. Her father's daughter, through and through.

'You know if you lie there much longer that baby will be born with vertigo,' Justine said as she went to the door.

Teresa squirmed on the *chaise-longue* and pouted, 'Dr Hubbatt said I must rest as much as possible. I'm not as strong as you, Justine, and this baby is important.'

'To whom?' Justine mumbled to herself as she kicked shut the drawing-room door after her.

She took the tray to the kitchen and started stacking the dirty crocks into the dishwasher.

'How is your sister this afternoon?' Janet the housekeeper asked as she came into the kitchen with a tray of tea things from the study where Richard was working.

'Suffering like some Gothic heroine,' Justine grinned wickedly. 'Anyone would think she was the first woman on earth having a baby. When I was in South America the women shambled off into the forest, birthed and went straight back to work with the newborn strapped to their backs.'

Janet smiled benignly. 'That wouldn't do for Miss Teresa, no, not at all.'

No, not at all, Justine grumbled to herself as she went upstairs to her bedroom. And she wasn't Miss Teresa any more, she was very much Madame Richard Peterson with delusions of grandeur like her husband. Justine was almost sickened by the way the two acted, forever trying to please her father. Teresa had been that way as a child but Justine had thought marriage would have cured her of the need to please when it wasn't necessary. Now there were two of them at it, Richard all the more sickening because his reasons were monetary. Now that he had married into the family he expected the business to be turned over to him.

Justine grinned to herself as she closed her bedroom door after her. Some hope; her father was too cute for that—though the smile slid from her face at the thought of the dinner party tonight. This was all Richard's idea, to wine and dine Max Benedict and probably throw his sister-in-law at his feet to get the contract he so desired and so go up another rung in her father's estimation.

To hell with all of them, Justine cursed as she pulled her portfolio out from the wardrobe. By rights she should sort through her clothes for something suitable to wear this evening. Not that Max Benedict would notice if she wore Versace's latest. The man had taste and style and it ran to his women and Justine had never been in the running, not with her looks nor with her talent, so what the devil did it matter how she looked tonight?

She spent the rest of the afternoon running nostalgically through her portfolio, and because Max Benedict was about to pop back into her life she couldn't help recalling how scornful he had been about her work when she had gone to him six months ago...

'I haven't much time, Miss Hammond—please be brief.' His blue eyes narrowed coldly then.

'Hammond... John Hammond's daughter? Yes, of course, my secretary said.'

He rubbed his forehead impatiently to add to how small he was already making her feel and though Justine was inwardly squirming that she had been forced to come to him because she had failed so dismally elsewhere and he was her very last resort she was eternally grateful he hadn't remembered that earlier embarrassing meeting.

'I... I'm sorry. I'm not in favour of nepotism but I knew you wouldn't see me if I just bowled in off the street.'

'Not in favour of nepotism,' he drawled sarcastically, 'yet you resort to it——'

'I had to!' Justine blurted, feeling herself going red in her desperation. But there was still some fight left. 'I... I thought you deserved first choice...' Oh, please don't let him see through my flattery-will-get-me-anywhere ruse. 'You are the biggest and the best and I thought I'd offer you sight of my work before I offered it to your competitors.'

Wrong! He had no competitors. He was the ultimate tycoon of magazine and book publishing. She had boobed and it was all hopeless. He would know she was trying to flatter him.

She darted forward and unclipped her portfolio and scattered her work across his desk before he could say anything more. A defeatist she was not.

'These are my own,' she ran on. 'I've been travelling for a couple of years. I worked my way through Europe, worked a ship to South America—even made Mexico. I took these photographs *en route*. I have others, by other photographers, to make up my photo library. I cover everything, human interest, flora and fauna...' Oh, God, he wasn't even looking at them, just staring at her as if she were a flea in his sumptuous office and he was considering calling in a pest controller.

'We have met before, haven't we?' he said quietly, holding her eyes with intensity. Then he smiled and Justine wasn't warmed by it but rather warned. 'Yes, it's coming back. We have met before—Munich, wasn't it?'

Hell, Munich was a far cry from Belgravia and he sure had a cutting way of putting a girl down yet again.

She shook her head. 'I'm sure I would have remembered if we had met before,' she braved and then smiled beguilingly. 'I've got one of those universal faces, I suppose; everyone thinks they've met me before.'

He smiled genuinely then and Justine wondered, just wondered if he did remember and was playing games with her.

'On the contrary, I'd say you had a unique face...'

Oh, yes, he was warming and so was Justine, warming and squirming and dying of embarrassment.

'A remarkable natural beauty that is rare these days——'

'Yes, well, that's beside the point,' she hurried on, interrupting him and shuffling her photographs. 'I'm sure you'll agree these are excellent and you can find a place for them and continue to use my photo library. I have thousands of transparencies. I offer a very comprehensive service...' Her voice trailed to a faint whisper as he picked up a handful and flicked through them hastily. Then he tossed them down on the desk and Justine's heart sank. She knew they were good but he appeared completely and utterly unimpressed.

'This isn't my department, you know. I employ people to do all this for me——'

'Yes, I know,' she interrupted again, desperate now. 'But I don't bother with the monkey when it's the organ grinder I want.' Oh, she could have bitten her tongue out. To compare this tall, dark, impressive, striking giant of a man to an organ grinder...

His brow rose darkly and suspiciously and he studied her from behind his desk as if now she had metamorphosed herself from flea to a poisonous spider, equally undesirable in his air space.

'Your work is good,' he said slowly and decisively and Justine's pulses began to race with hope, 'but nothing out of the ordinary, I'm afraid.'

Justine stared at him in disbelief. Nothing out of the ordinary? They were original, fresh with a different approach, artistic, stunning...a thousand other adjectives. They were *superb*! How could he think they weren't?

'You...you haven't looked at them properly——'

'I've seen enough to know I can't use them. We already use several excellent photo libraries.' He stood up then and straightened his waistcoat and for a second she thought he was going to draw back his crisp white cuff and look at his watch, the ultimate of wasting-my-time put-downs. But he didn't, he didn't have to because the glazed, uninterested look in his eyes, clouding them to grey now, was enough.

Biting her lower lip, Justine lowered her dark lashes and shuffled the prints back into her portfolio case. This was the end and she knew it. The end of all her dreams, because she couldn't last another day desperately trying to sell the work she had been stacking up on her travels. She had a superb collection of work and had been convinced they would be snapped up and now she was disillusioned and tired and thoroughly put down.

'Well, this is your loss not mine,' she thrust back at him as she stared at him defiantly.

He simply shrugged and drawled, 'Yes, very probably. Perhaps you'll fare better with my so-called competitors.' There was just a trace of mockery to that and Justine rallied against it so strongly that her next words came out so forcefully she even shocked herself.

'You wouldn't recognise talent if it hit you between the eyes, which it just has, incidentally. Trouble with people like you is that you think you are just too big——'

'Thank you, Miss Hammond, don't call again. My time is precious.'

This time the cuff did go back and the yellow gold of his very expensive watch hit Justine between the eyes. It dazzled and stung and drove her failure so completely home to her that she felt sick with it. Always, but always, she had been able to hold her own, but this one attempt at starting her very own business just wasn't coming off. It occurred to her that because she was John Hammond's daughter he probably thought she wasn't taking it all seriously. It was just a whim on her part. Nearly, very nearly, she pleaded with him to reconsider, to try and explain that she was serious about her work and if she didn't get some more clients *now* it was all going to be a horrible failure. But pride held her back. Max Benedict didn't want to hear a hard-luck story from a rich man's daughter.

Justine tucked her portfolio under her arm, turned and walked towards the door and didn't look back, but her ears were in tune and she heard the click of the phone as he picked it up, asking his secretary to put him through to a Cassandra Donoghue.

Justine Hammond didn't exist, it was the Cassandras of the world who mattered to him, and there were many of them, so she'd read in all the tabloids. So incensed by his cold dismissal of her and, by comparison, the soft tones he used on the phone, before she had even left the room she did something extremely childish, extremely stupid and extremely wilful. There was a cute little pot of African violets on a small table by the door. Without giving it a thought, Justine scooped it up as she opened the door. She turned and in a fury of rejection she hurled it. Max Benedict ducked. The pot hit the wall. Justine fled, slamming the door behind her.

For a long, long time she couldn't get rid of that image of him as he had ducked. Shocked disbelief as the pot hurtled towards him and then something else, a curious sort of look, one that to this day she still hadn't fathomed. Obviously no one had ever hurled a pot of African violets at his head before!

And now he was coming to dinner tonight and she would have to face him, and poor old Teresa and Richard were going to get a shock, because Max Benedict hadn't remembered the first time he had met Justine Hammond but he couldn't fail to remember the second time—and there was a full moon tonight.

CHAPTER TWO

IT SEEMED appropriate to wear the African-violet-coloured silk dress she had acquired on her travels. Justine was in a rebellious mood as ever but as she slipped it over her head she felt guilty for wanting to stab at him this way, especially as it was so important to 'be nice' to him tonight.

Depression swamped her as the fine silk fluttered around her knees. Her father's company was in trouble and here she was wanting to give Max Benedict a vengeful reminder of the pot-throwing incident when she should be thinking of her father instead of being so childish. But the trouble was that her thoughts on Max weren't childish: they were very adult. Once she'd had a teenage crush on him, all on the strength of that one meeting in Belgravia. She remembered the sleepless nights that had gone hand in hand with unrequited love but she had got over it. Not so easy to get over was his second rejection of her, made all the more painful by the fact that he had rejected her talent that time. In a way she had coped with that also, but now he was about to step into her life again and that seemed like some sort of grim punishment. How would she feel when she saw him tonight? That she couldn't answer till it happened, but it worried her. A welling-up of that old attraction was something she didn't need at this most vulnerable stage in her life when her thoughts needed to concentrate on trying to make a living for herself and getting out from under her sister's and brother-in-law's feet.

Her eyes narrowed worriedly as Teresa swept into the bedroom.

'Well, I'm glad to see you have something decent to wear. Just button that mouth of yours and speak when you're spoken to and we might get somewhere tonight,' Teresa stated frostily as she went to the window to see if Max Benedict's arrival was imminent.

'Is it really so very important?' Justine asked quietly and sombrely, realising that her sister was very tense.

'Of course it's important, Justine.' Teresa turned then and looked at her. 'If Richard doesn't get this contract from Benedict it could be the end of Daddy's empire. He's worn himself ragged lately and so has Richard and the strain on me has been immense. If anything happens to this baby...'

It would all be her fault, Justine thought painfully, just as she had been blamed for everything in her childhood. It had always been Justine's fault. Of course this really wasn't her fault, the trouble the company was in, but she sympathised and deep down she knew this rebellious streak of hers would have to be curbed tonight. She would 'be nice', she wouldn't say anything out of line, she would be the height of decorum and then she would retire to bed and gnash her teeth to her heart's content.

'I won't let you down, Teresa,' Justine said softly.

'You'd better not, Sis,' Teresa huffed as she straightened and smoothed the velvet curtains before crossing the room. She turned at the door.

'Because you'll have to face the wrath of my husband if you do!'

'My knees are trembling.' Justine couldn't resist.

'And cut that out and put your hair up or something; you look wild and unkempt with it down. Make an effort, Justine. You're home now and your wild days are over.' She slammed the door shut.

Justine reluctantly did as she'd ordered, swept her Titian hair up to the top of her head and glared at herself in the mirror. No matter how hard she tried, sophistication was always just out of reach. Spirals of wispy curls escaped the clasp and drizzled around the nape of her neck.

'Sorry, that's the best I can do,' she murmured as she took one last look.

She was coming down the curving oak stairway when she heard the car on the drive. Justine's heart stilled and then her long legs raced her into the drawing-room where Teresa and Richard were waiting expectantly, Teresa languishing once again on the *chaise-longue*, looking quite pale and beautiful in flowing oyster-cream chiffon, Richard standing stiffly and expectantly by the fireplace.

'That sounds like him,' Richard stated, needlessly to Justine's ears as no other guests had been invited. But she supposed he was nervous. Smoothing his brown hair and straightening his bowtie, he cleared his throat and went to greet Max Benedict in the hall of the rambling manor.

Justine took up a position by the window, as far away from the Adam-style fireplace where a huge log fire blazed as was possible. On such a bitter night they would all gather there for pre-dinner drinks and she really wasn't a part of all this, just here to make up the foursome...

Except there wasn't going to be a foursome, Justine thought wildly as voices drifted in from the echoey hall. There was another voice out there... Oh, good grief, Max Benedict had brought someone with him... a woman!

The same thought had hit Teresa and she struggled to her feet, uttered a muted curse and then said wildly to Justine, 'I didn't think he'd bring anyone! Janet will have a fit—she's only set up for four——'

'You don't need me, then,' Justine said quickly, seeing her chance to escape and at the same time experiencing a huge rush of disappointment that thoroughly astonished her.

'You're the whole point,' Teresa seethed, making strides across the room to the door that connected with the dining-room. 'I'll just slip out to Janet to tell her——'

'Just a minute,' Justine croaked, going after her and catching her at the door. She clutched at her sister's arm, her pulses racing at what Teresa had just let slip. 'What do you mean, I'm the whole point?'

'This isn't the time, Justine,' Teresa cried. 'Just hold the fort till I get back.' With that she wrenched her arm away and as she disappeared out of one door Richard and the dinner guests came in from the one off the hall.

Justine swung round, heart racing so wildly that it drummed in her ears. The first person who stepped into the room was a beautiful brunette in a bruised-raspberry-coloured creation that clung where it touched, which was practically all over. Max Benedict followed and his eyes met Justine's over the shoulder of his lovely companion. He looked directly at her and he wasn't in the least surprised or shocked to see her standing there and Justine was quite taken aback by that lack of disbelief. Then several things dawned on her at once and in confusion she stood rooted to the spot as Richard made the introductions.

She knew it all now. Richard, in his eagerness to cement this contract, was using her as bait, but what he didn't know was that Max Benedict was so sharp he could cut his own throat without trying and he had seen through this ruse, hence the lovely lady with him tonight. He was calling Richard's bluff because being partnered with Justine Hammond for the evening was the last thing he wanted or needed in his life. One small cloud of uncertainty misted that thinking though. Surely Teresa would have told Richard how disenchanted Benedict had been with her the first time they had met? Of course nobody else knew about the other disastrous meeting, only she and Max Benedict knew about that, but maybe, just hopefully maybe, he might have forgotten.

Suddenly Max was lifting her hand and brushing a kiss across the back of it and those devastating blue eyes of his locked into hers and he murmured for her ears only, 'Violet looks better on you than me.'

He hadn't forgotten, that was evident. Justine fought the rising tide of crimson embarrassment that threatened her neck and face. She forced a smile and then the smile slid from her face as she noticed for the first time, the leather thong that looped over his shoulder and around his neck to hold his right arm stiffly at an angle against his dinner-jacket. She had no chance to question it in mind or verbally as Teresa swept back into the room, to gush her welcomes over Benedict and his partner.

Drinks were poured and Richard and Teresa and the bruised-raspberry lady, Beverley, vied for verbal air space while Justine and Max Benedict exchanged furtive glances.

'It would have to be the polo field, wouldn't it?' tinkled Bev, as she insisted on being called. 'He couldn't have cracked up his arm in a mundane game of table tennis, could he?'

Here was a lady who knew Max Benedict through and through, thought Justine with admiration for the bubbly brunette as she sparkled on, explaining the reason for that right arm of his strapped to his chest.

'One more operation and he should be fighting fit once again. Till then, the poor baby has to take one day at a time.'

Max Benedict's brows came up and his eyes sparkled with humour for only Justine as he lifted his glass to his lips.

He's loving all this, Justine thought critically, all the wounded-soldier bit, lapping up Bev's attention and obvious adoration. He probably doesn't care an organ grinder's monkey for her; he's just using her to get at me and to pamper his grotesque ego.

Max disengaged his eyes from Justine's and her relief was heady.

'And Bev has been a tower of strength to me these past months since the accident,' Max offered. 'She drives for me when my chauffeur is off duty, cuts up my food for me, does everything for me that I'm not able to do with one hand.'

This was all said very tongue-in-cheek but by the serious expressions on everyone's faces Justine seemed to be the only one who thought it all amusing.

'How very admirable,' Richard blustered, glancing approvingly at Bev.

Teresa glowered. Justine smiled and sipped her drink and mused that this dinner party might be fun after all. She couldn't wait to see the precious Bev cutting Max Benedict's food into bite-sized pieces. She couldn't wait to see if she fed him too.

There was the inevitable division of conversation during the pre-dinner-drinks time. Richard monopolised Max on one side of the fireplace, while Bev draped herself next to Teresa, who now graced the wide sofa in front of the roaring fire, and looked suitably interested in baby talk, and Justine had never felt more alone in her life. She was excess to requirements now that Max had turned up with his female minder and she felt awkward and ill at ease and wondered if anyone would notice if she disappeared.

Teresa read her thoughts and glowered yet again and whispered to her as they went through to the dining-room after Janet had announced that dinner was served, 'Your hair is all over the place, Justine——'

'I think it looks very charming,' Max Benedict said, turning to them as they followed him and

Richard into the dining-room. Teresa looked mildly squashed and went forward into the room to seat Beverley at the oval dining-table.

For a moment Justine and Max hung back by the door.

'I don't need you to fight my battles,' Justine seethed under her breath, despising him for making a comment like that and making her feel even more ill at ease.

'I know you don't,' he whispered back. 'You're quite able to fight your own but what you're not able to do is recognise a compliment when you hear one.'

'Oh.'

'Sit here next to Bev,' Richard ordered rather than suggested to Max.

Justine positively felt the stiffening of Max next to her. He obviously didn't like taking orders.

'Seeing as this is such a pleasant *social* occasion——' Max laid emphasis on the word social, which made Justine think again that Max knew exactly what the purpose of this dinner party was and wasn't too at ease with it '—I'd like to give Bev a break. I'm sure Justine wouldn't mind acting as my right-hand helper for the evening, would you, Justine?'

He gave Justine such a dazzling smile that she nearly melted but sense ruled and suddenly she was aware of a very tricky situation here. Games were being played, but so far Justine wasn't sure who the players were and who was playing against whom. Bev certainly looked put out by the suggestion and Justine wondered just how intense their relationship was and if Max was playing everyone off against each other.

'Your wish is our command,' Richard crawled, and pulled out a chair for Justine.

So here she was, seated at Max's right and expected to help him with his food, which was going to be some test of character, she supposed. Already she was sharply aware of the closeness of him. She felt the heat of his body, was very aware of the sharp cut of his evening suit, the softness of his silk shirt against his chest, the faint scent of his after-shave that was even more delicious an aroma than the soup Janet was serving.

'Well, the soup doesn't need cutting,' Justine stated somewhat sarcastically.

Teresa took a sharp intake of breath and glowered across the table at Justine, who simply glared back because the anticipated fun of the evening was fast developing into a huge embarrassment.

'My roll needs breaking up, though,' Max said, his voice so loaded with mischief that Justine knew this was a punishment for the African violets. 'Would you be so kind, Justine?'

Richard dared her not to be and Justine wondered if Max was picking up on these exchanged glances. There was certainly an atmosphere that was not conducive to a 'pleasant social occasion' even though everyone was battling for politeness.

Justine obliged by breaking his roll into small pieces for him and couldn't resist saying, 'I used to do this for the ducks when I was a child.'

Max laughed lightly and Bev opened her lovely red mouth and let out a scream of laughter, but Teresa and Richard were not amused and it seemed to Justine that from then on it was downhill all the way.

'Yes, it aches miserably most of the time,' Max later responded to Teresa's query about his arm. 'I've lost the use of three fingers due to the pressure on the nerves in my elbow and now my thumb is seizing up too but they can't operate again till the first setting has been given a chance to heal.'

'That's private medicine for you,' Justine commented.

'Justine!' Richard thundered.

Justine paused with her soup spoon midway between her bowl and her mouth and widened her green eyes innocently at her brother-in-law's outrage.

'That sort of comment is out of order, Justine,' Richard went on abrasively.

'It was just that, a comment, Richard,' Justine countered, placing her spoon carefully at the side of her bowl, her appetite gone now. 'Something to liven the evening up.' And boy did it need a shot in the arm!

'I'd like to hear more of those comments,' Max said quietly, and Richard's mouth thinned.

Justine shrugged. 'I assume the first operation wasn't a success and something went wrong which necessitates further surgery. I'm not saying that never happens with the NHS but I'm inclined to think that private sector of medicine can afford to make mistakes——'

'Implying that they do to generate more business?' Max asked in amusement, and then immediately went on, 'An interesting theory; one that hadn't occurred to me. It seems that I'm paying for somebody's mistake in more than just pain, then.' He was grinning by the time he'd finished and

Justine knew that he'd taken her comments just as they were meant to be taken, light-heartedly, something to get this dinner party moving. She smiled back.

'Justine's childish conjectures spring from her own bitterness with the world at the moment, though her politics have always been suspect,' Teresa put in unmercifully. 'She never has known her place in society.'

It was a biting, cutting, snobby retort and Justine smarted under its severity. She sat back as everyone carried on eating and held her hands tightly clenched in her lap.

'Are you bitter with the world?' Max asked softly at her side.

Richard took up the question as if it had been directed at him not Justine. 'Justine thought she had a business head on her shoulders and has just found out she hasn't the acumen for it. She's out of work at the moment and though we sympathise she really ought to realise that nothing can be achieved by living with her pretty little head in the clouds——'

Oh, God, I want to die, Justine thought miserably.

'She started a silly little photo library that hadn't a leg to stand on from the start,' Richard went on, seemingly unaware of how deeply he was putting her down. 'We told her but she wouldn't listen——'

'Has she ever?' Teresa thrust in. 'I do hope you like game, Max. From the estate, of course. Richard raised ten thousand pheasant last year——'

'And lost three hundred chicks because they were put out too early and perished in a storm,' Justine husked under her breath as Janet clattered around with silver salvers behind them, waiting to clear the soup plates and serve the next course.

No one heard her breathy misery but Max, and he turned to her slightly and under the corner of the damask tablecloth pressed his leg against hers. Justine in astonishment raised her eyes from her lap and glanced at him and then glowered and shifted her leg as far away from him as was possible. She doubted if that was a sympathetic shove for the chicks that had perished, but more a gesture of support for her after Richard and Teresa had so successfully dashed her pride. Support nor sympathy from him did she need.

The conversation droned on without Justine making any more comments; she just sipped her wine and studied the faces around her, wishing she had a camera with her to snap some of the strained expressions. Beverley had started the evening well but now was looking as if boredom was soaking in, apart from the wary looks she was giving Justine occasionally, not trusting her to look after Max as well as she obviously could.

In grim silence Justine helped Max with the next course, cutting the pheasant, though it was so tender it practically broke itself apart. The vegetables were tender enough for him to deal with himself—she handed him back his fork and their fingers brushed in the exchange. Warm hand, cold heart, she pondered and mechanically started to eat as the conversation drifted to places that were out of her region.

'You're not saying much,' Max murmured next to her as Bev, who had rallied, bubbled on about the antique furniture that adorned the sumptuous dining-room, engaging Richard and Teresa in their favourite subjects, ostentation and the monetary worth of every piece Bev admired.

'I was always taught not to speak with my mouth full,' Justine said after swallowing.

'So you do know how to behave when you want to,' he teased lightly.

'Yes, and how to misbehave when necessary,' she told him pointedly. She poured him more wine.

He smiled, getting the point immediately. 'I'm sorry your business failed——'

Teresa had the enviable knack of being able to follow more than one conversation at the same time and she leaned forward and directed to Max, 'Please don't encourage her, Max. Justine has had some wild ideas in her time——'

'I'm all for free enterprise, Teresa,' Max interrupted firmly. 'And I'm sure if Justine failed it wasn't due to lack of talent. The economic climate is anathema to small businesses at the moment.'

'I couldn't agree more.' Richard spoke up, now seeing that Justine was getting far more support than he had anticipated from the mega-tycoon and abruptly moving sides. 'Of course, Justine is very talented but——'

Teresa wasn't so convinced and, being programmed to put Justine down from an early age, she couldn't give up now.

'But Justine hasn't a business head,' she finished for her husband.

Justine blanked off then. She could see what was happening now. Her sister was crushed because Max had turned up with another woman so there was no point in pushing Justine on to him. As far as Teresa was concerned her ruse had failed before it had got going. So putting down Justine Hammond was the next course. Secretly Justine couldn't bear this put-down from her sister and brother-in-law, especially as she was still feeling so vulnerable over the loss of her business, but what was worse was Max suddenly standing up for her when it was his cold dismissal of her talent that had started the decline in the first place. If only he had used her agency...

Justine tuned in again to the conversation when the dessert was being presented.

'The meringue looks delicious,' she heard Max say politely to Janet as she offered him a choice of desserts. 'This could be difficult,' he said to Justine. 'Would you do the honours?'

Justine stared in dismay at the crisp mound of Janet's mouth-watering peaked meringue in front of him. Why, oh, why, had he had to pick that one? She knew from past experience that Janet's meringues, though quite delicious, were a disaster to eat tidily.

Nervously she picked up a spoon and fork and tried tentatively to break it into pieces for him. She could tell by the vibes he gave off that he was enjoying her struggle and when she glanced at him sideways she saw a wide grin spread across his face. She also noted everyone else glowering at her suspiciously. Bev glowered more than the others, surprisingly, but her expression was tinged with just a hint of jealousy, Justine supposed. This was a very intimate thing to do for someone with only the use of one arm and somehow the oozing fresh cream and the crushed strawberry sorbet that made up the rest of the dessert seemed to add a certain eroticism to the whole procedure... and a very grave risk.

'Oh, my God!' Justine gasped as a piece of the crispy meringue shot from the plate to the front of Max Benedict's beautiful silk evening shirt. Adhered to it was a great blob of cream and a smudge of the strawberry sorbet and the lot slid down his shirt front in Technicolor slow motion and settled obligingly on the bulge of one of his thighs.

Justine started to shake then with suppressed laughter. Max sat as stiff as a board and the aghast looks of all were too much for Justine. With a stifled splutter she burst out laughing, snatched at her napkin and grabbed at the offending piece of meringue.

Max's hand clasped over hers and held it and the squashy napkin firmly against his thigh and she felt the tremor of mirth from him vibrate up her arm like an electric shock. Astonished, she looked at his grim features but they didn't give anything away.

'Justine!' Teresa screeched and leapt to her feet and propelled herself round the table. 'You are *absolutely* impossible! How could you be so damned careless?'

Eyes as black as thunderclouds, she was about to wrench the napkin away when Max said quickly.

'It's quite all right, Teresa—in fact I'm beginning to enjoy it.'

Teresa went faintly red, Bev looked daggers, Richard pursed his lips and Justine sat immobile, the laughter gone, Max's hand still firmly clasped over hers. Her heart was racing at his touch but she didn't allow herself to enjoy it because this was Max Benedict's way of scoring off his opponents. He was hating this doomed dinner party. Why he'd accepted the invitation she couldn't imagine. Quite obviously he had nothing in common with any of them.

'If... if you're sure...' Teresa muttered, giving her husband a stricken look and then receiving the unspoken order to sit down and shut up.

Justine tensed her fingers and, twisting out of Max's grasp, she rubbed at the cream on his black evening trousers and then attacked the mess on his shirt-front. Without looking at him she muttered her profuse apologies.

'I'm getting used to you hurling things at me. I wonder what it will be next?' he said for all to hear.

To anyone not knowing what he was referring to that was a mysterious thing to say and he knew it. Games again, thought Justine as she tossed the dirty napkin on the serving sideboard behind her. She began to enter into the spirit of the evening.

'That's for you to find out,' she teased and smiled sweetly at Max and then to everyone watching this exchange with interest.

Suddenly, Richard, looking flushed with embarrassment, accelerated the conversation to its intended path.

'To get back to what we were talking about earlier, Max. It would be my great pleasure to escort you to the Hammond Mill in Scotland and show you our product from source...'

Teresa and Bev went back to their verbal *Antiques Roadshow* and Justine consumed her crème caramel and half listened to Richard trying to persuade Max to do something he didn't want to.

'We could fly up next week——'

'I don't fly, I'm afraid, Richard. I have a pathological fear of it.'

'Oh!' came a surprised Richard.

Oh! came inwardly from a surprised Justine as she listened with acute interest now. So Max Benedict wasn't macho man after all. He had a flaw in that mega-man image he exuded. *Poor baby* was afraid of flying.

'And I'm not keen on rail travel either,' Max put in before Richard suggested it.

'Oh, dear,' muttered Richard, going down like a tyre with a slow puncture.

Justine smiled to herself as she drained the last of her wine. Poor Richard—and then the smile faded from Justine's lips: poor Daddy.

'So how do you travel, Max?' Justine squirmed into the conversation, gauging her voice down to light-hearted sarcasm as she added, 'Jet-propelled skate-board?'

As that came out all other conversation seized and the inevitable glowering looks were back with a vengeance.

'Now there's a thought,' Max said with a good humour which brought the colour back to Teresa's cheeks. 'Actually I favour driving.' He gave a small dismissive shrug of his wide shoulders. 'But sadly that pleasure is denied me at the moment with this wretched arm.'

'You mentioned a chauffeur,' Justine said. 'Surely he could drive you up to Scotland?' She could see Richard losing all this and though she wasn't one of his greatest admirers she thought she ought to do something for the sake of the family business.

'He's on leave at the moment,' Max came back with, turning slightly to see how that would fall on Justine's ears.

She held his cool look and defied it with more sarcasm. 'Surely you carry a spare about your person?'

'This isn't a time for frivolity,' Teresa grazed at her sister.

'I . . . I could . . .' Richard began.

Max's left hand came up. 'I wouldn't dream of it, Richard. You're a busy man, I'm sure, and didn't you say you were off to Europe later in the week?'

Oh, God, couldn't her brother-in-law see that Max Benedict just wasn't interested?

'Yes, but . . .' Richard was floundering, grasping at straws now, twisting his mouth in agony trying to get the words out.

'You could put the European trip off, Richard,' Teresa suggested quickly.

Richard gave his wife an agonised look and Justine guessed that the Europe trip was equally important as trying to squeeze this contract out of Benedict.

Max leaned back in his seat in such a calculated way that all eyes were suddenly on him. 'I must say that your propositions are interesting to me, though,' he said slowly, 'and a visit to the mill in Scotland would help me make a decision——'

'Then of course you must put off the trip to Europe,' Teresa interjected firmly, her green eyes warning her husband.

'I... I suppose...'

'I've a better idea,' Max said quietly and he lifted his head and gazed directly at each of them in turn and then settled on Beverley's eyes. Hers suddenly lit up in expectation and then as swiftly went out like a light as Max's idea hit the heavy air space over everyone's head. 'Why doesn't Justine drive me up to Scotland?'

CHAPTER THREE

IT HUNG there like a helium balloon, that silly, silly suggestion.

Justine laughed, albeit nervously, as her sister and brother-in-law looked equally astounded by the very idea.

'You don't even know if I can drive!' she protested.

'But I do,' Max said quietly.

Suddenly Bev stood up from the table. Justine noticed that her exuberance had faded.

'Will you excuse me? The little girls' room,' she said in a small voice.

Teresa went with her to show her the way, so stunned by Max's suggestion that she was reduced to near silence as she ushered Bev out of the room.

Janet came in from the other door to say that coffee and brandy were waiting in the drawing-room and could Richard take a phone call in the study?

Justine rounded on Max Benedict as soon as he closed the drawing-room door after them both. She faced him, eyes blazing furiously. 'How dare you do that? How dare you play people off against each other? How dare you make such a ridiculous suggestion?'

'I thought it amused you—nothing much else has this dire evening,' he said quietly, going to the sofa table and pouring two coffees with his good hand.

'You forget the meringue episode. Now that *was* funny,' she fumed sarcastically. 'And I laughed just now because the idea of me acting as your chauffeur is ludicrous——'

'Why should the idea of you driving me to Scotland be ludicrous? From what I gather from the conversation tonight, you aren't doing much else with your time at the moment.'

That was a bit below the belt and Justine acted with the dismissive contempt it deserved. 'What I do with my time is beside the point!' she flamed. 'You were playing games with everyone tonight, playing good honest human beings off against each other. That . . . that Beverley . . . she was quite obviously expecting you to ask her to drive you up and you smashed her down . . . in front of everyone. You used her . . . you got her to drive you here tonight——'

'I don't use people, Justine——'

'You just did! You used all of us! You made Richard squirm . . . you irritated my sister . . . you've devastated Bev——'

He turned on her then, blue eyes steely with sudden anger. Even with his bad arm strapped to his chest he looked formidably arrogant. 'Let's get a few points straight before you hurl another potted plant at my head,' he raged. 'Beverley and I have an understanding——'

'Sure. It damned well looked like it!' Justine rallied, not to be put down as easily as he'd put her down twice before in her life.

'Listen to me,' he breathed ruthlessly, stepping towards her threateningly, 'because if you don't I'll walk out of here now and you and your wimpy brother-in-law and your father's business will get nothing from me, do you hear? Nothing!'

Justine held on to her defiance till it hurt to do so. Her finger came up and she pointed it meanly at him.

'And don't threaten me, Max Benedict. You're talking to one Hammond who doesn't have the need to grovel. I'm not a part of this. Sure, I care about my father's business, but I don't care enough to be nice to *you* for it!'

'So, you're quite prepared to sit back and see your own father lose a lifetime's work because you're not prepared to be nice to someone? I'm beginning to see why your sister and brother-in-law treat you like a rebellious child, because you are one.'

He turned away from her then and tried to pour himself a brandy from the crystal decanter and cursed loudly as the stopper jammed and he couldn't quite make it with his one hand.

'Let me do that before you shatter it,' Justine said impatiently and snatched the decanter out of his reach. It was then she noticed the clenching of his injured hand as he tried desperately to work his numb fingers. Her eyes went from the lame numbness of those fingers to the despair in his eyes and her heart bleeped with sympathy. For this to happen to a man such as he must be particularly unbearable.

'I'm sorry,' she murmured softly. 'It must be hell for you.'

'It is,' he admitted quietly. 'Try strapping your own right arm to your chest for a few days and see how you fare.'

'Quite, but don't trawl for sympathy from me, Max. I've seen kids with no arms at all fighting for survival on the streets in Rio and making it.'

'OK, OK, point taken,' he said impatiently. 'You are some hard lady.'

'And you are some hard man where Beverley is concerned,' she countered, not to be denied digging at that, bad arm or not.

He sat down on the sofa in front of the fire and took the brandy she offered.

Justine moved a side-table closer to him and put his coffee down on it.

He looked up at her and met her green eyes full on. 'We are not lovers and we never have been. We have a good friendship and a good relationship and——'

'And she wishes it were more,' Justine finished for him, pulling a pouffe up to the fireside and sitting on the edge of it to drink her brandy and coffee.

'You can tell?' he said quietly.

Justine nodded without saying anything.

Max was quiet for a moment as if pondering that thought. 'It's a recent thing,' he said at last. 'Since the accident. She likes to mother me.'

'Huh, I can't imagine your *mother* mothering you!' Justine retorted waspishly.

'Careful, Justine, you're being childish again.'

'I'm in good company, then.'

'Don't you ever ease off?'

She swallowed a mouthful of brandy and quickly picked up her coffee to ease the burning liquid down. 'I'm not willing to mother you and softly, softly you just because you're partially disabled at the moment. It's a temporary inconvenience for you and you'll live, but if you insist on me driving you up to Scotland you could end up with another cracked-up arm for your trouble.'

'Why should I insist on you driving me? It was only a suggestion, you know.'

Again she felt that plop of disappointment. Dear God, hadn't she learnt anything from this man?

'Will you insist?' she asked quietly, staring at the fire rather than daring to see the cold dismissal in his eyes to accompany another put-down.

'I could easily insist but I doubt you'd take much notice of any orders I gave out. I'll use emotional blackmail on you, though—I'm not above a bit of that.'

He was mocking her now but she could take it.

'You're just a bastard, then, just a shade below my creepy brother-in-law who arranged this embarrassing dinner party tonight. Anyway, I've already told you, I can't be swayed that way.'

'So you don't love your father?'

She looked at him then, her mouth grim set, her eyes only a shade darker than the green silk of the sofa he was sitting on. 'I adore him,' she told him in a soft whisper. 'But I don't have to prove it by jumping to your every whim. I leave that to my sister who thinks she has to prove her worth in the only way she can, a monetary way. Daddy knows I adore him. We rarely see eye to eye, I've always been wilful—I'm sure he loves me for it even in his exasperation.'

'And yet you're quite willing to stand by and see your father lose his business and do nothing to try and help?'

Justine looked at him shrewdly. 'And me driving you to Scotland will help, will it?' She smiled wryly and cradled the brandy glass in her two hands while he swirled his in his one hand. 'I give you more credit for your good sense than you do yourself, Max Benedict. You'll put your paper contract with whomsoever you choose and dinner parties and fawning and spawning won't make a scrap of difference, so my driving you to Scotland is a total waste of time.'

Max smiled across at her. 'And there was I feeling sorry for you because your family were putting you down so badly tonight. You have talent all right, Justine Hammond, and you have a good business head on your shoulders.'

'Wrong. I won't deny I have talent but my business failed and it wouldn't have done if I had a good business head, so don't try flattering me now when you were so dismissive of me six months ago. And don't waste your pity on me because I don't need it. You put me down once but you'll never get the chance again.'

'Is that why you heaved that pot of African violets at my head?'

She held his eyes again. Green against blue. 'Is that why you made that ridiculous suggestion tonight, to pay me back?'

He laughed. 'Not at all. I was paying your family back, as it happens. Richard is a bore and I wanted to see his face when you refused.'

'So you were playing games tonight?'

'Weren't we all?'

'Probably,' Justine murmured, averting her eyes to the fire again. Here she was, trying to convince herself and her sister that she disliked him intently and feeling shudders of disappointment trickling down her spine at the thought that he wasn't insisting on her driving him. And he wouldn't, she knew that now. It was all just a wind-up game. But, even knowing all that, she couldn't help feeling the magnetism that had drawn her to him years back. He was a very attractive man. Even with that ridiculous arm strapped to his chest he was a power to be reckoned with. It didn't make her feel softer towards him though. She wasn't a hard lady, not at all—she knew that his arm would get better and this was just a temporary disability for him. No, her feelings weren't powered by pity this time. Feelings? What feelings? She didn't really know; all she did know for sure was the existence of excitement within her when she was facing him. Twice and probably three times he had put her down and each time she had felt that strange, almost masochistic excitement that he aroused in her. Part of it was the battle element he provoked in her, making her so furious with him that it was almost uncontrollable, but another part cried out to know the tender, sensuous part of his nature, *if* it existed.

'More brandy?' she asked quietly.

He nodded and stretched out his empty goblet to her and she took it without asking what his last slave had died from.

'Teresa and Bev are taking a long time and Richard's phone call is going on a bit. Do you get the distinct impression that we are purposely being left alone?' she asked as she poured the brandies and took them back to the fireside.

'That was the whole point of this evening, wasn't it?'

'Was it?'

'Didn't you know?' he asked softly.

Justine sat down by the fireside, this time curling herself on the rug in front of the fire, gathering her silk dress around her legs. She turned her face towards him and looked at him with knowing eyes. 'I guessed so. Teresa said I had to be nice to you and then when you arrived you didn't seem surprised to see me.'

'I wasn't surprised. When Richard called to invite me he made a point of mentioning you, an express point. It rather raised my suspicions that he wasn't above using a beautiful member of his family to get what he wanted—my yearly paper contract which is up for review.'

'Sort of corporate prostitution,' Justine suggested drily, ignoring the compliment he had slipped in. She sighed. He really was a creep, that brother-in-law of hers.

Max frowned. 'I don't play those sorts of games.'

'Nor I.'

'I'm glad to hear that.'

Justine smiled, the brandy really warming her and putting her resistance way down low. She turned her gaze back to the fire and murmured, 'And you brought Bev for protection?'

'Not at all. I too can fight my own battles, but in my circles when a dinner invitation is issued it includes a partner unless otherwise stated, and Richard didn't otherwise state.'

Justine wasn't too sure about that explanation but she didn't pursue it as he went on. 'Of course now I realise I wasn't expected to bring a partner, hence the sudden turnabout when your family started digging at you. I got the feeling they wouldn't have done if it had just been the four of us.' He paused, causing Justine to look at him again. His eyes weren't so blue, warmed by the reflection of the fire they looked a soft grey now. 'I apologise for that——'

Justine shrugged. 'It's not for you to apologise.'

'I feel slightly responsible nevertheless. You suffered because I did rather scupper their plans for the evening.'

'Yes, you did,' she agreed softly. 'But don't worry about me, I'm used to being berated. It happens in families and always appears far worse than it really is to outsiders.' She grinned then, impishly. 'What Richard and Teresa didn't know when they planned all this was that six months ago I heaved a poor defenceless pot of violets at your head.' She sighed. 'You know I cried over that afterwards.'

Max looked grave. 'I'm sorry. If I'd known how badly your business was going——'

'You still would have done what you did,' Justine interrupted and waved a small hand dismissively at him. 'Business is business. I understand—correction, I *understood*...' She was feeling very mellow now; in fact if she drank any more of this heady cognac she would be in danger of being slightly tipsy. 'And I didn't shed tears over your dismissal. I cried because you ducked and I missed and it was a terrible thing to do to a beautiful African violet!'

They were laughing when Richard blustered into the drawing-room, effusing apologies as the fountains of Rome effused litres of water.

'So sorry, so sorry about that, Max. There's no let-up in the business world, is there? Let me pour you another brandy.'

Creepy-crawly, mused Justine as she struggled to her feet, swaying slightly, and Max, who was already on his feet, reaching out with his good arm to steady her. Justine relished the contact, wanted more, that whole good arm of his to snuggle her into him. She hiccuped, covered her mouth with the back of her hand and grinned stupidly at her creepy-crawly bother-in-law... brother-in-law.

'No, thank you, Richard. I've had quite enough and so, apparently, has Justine. Where is Beverley?'

'Still upstairs with Teresa. She's showing her the Georgian sewing-box her grandmother left her——'

Victorian, Justine mouthed to Max, and he grinned and Justine covered her mouth again and giggled behind her hand.

'Thank you so much for your hospitality, Richard. The food was mouthwatering and it's been an enlightening evening. I'll be in touch on Monday to finalise the arrangements for Justine to drive me up to Scotland...'

The giggles went. Justine's mouth fell open. Richard beamed.

'It'll be a long drive but I'm sure Justine is very capable...'

Justine's mouth gaped wider. Richard nodded enthusiastically.

'It will necessitate several overnight stops, I'm afraid. I tire easily with this wretched arm, but I don't foresee any problems...'

Justine's heart began to race furiously. Richard was still nodding like one of those stuffed dogs in the back of a car.

'Most kind of Justine to accept my suggestion so graciously. She's a credit to the Hammond family.'

'Yes, yes, well, we always knew that,' enthused Richard. 'I'll go and call the girls.' He strode out of the room, a definite lift to his steps.

Justine turned on Max. 'You...you... bast——'

Max Benedict's good arm lashed out and caught her round the waist and with the power of four pairs of very good hands he clasped her to him, locking her stiffened body against his own. His mouth powered away the last vestige of her verbal insult in a kiss that stunned all fight from her. Her head swam with the crushing feeling of his lips on hers. Hot, forceful—ecstatic. They lingered, moved, caressed, shook her to the very roots of her being. And, as weak and senseless and as dizzy as she was, she recognised only one reasoning. This man was tricky. Dangerously tricky. He played games and he never came out the loser. She had warmed to him, let the brandy and the glowing warmth of the fire loosen her emotions till she could almost trust him and now he had slammed her down once again and gone right over her head and told a huge lie to her brother-in-law. She had *not* accepted his suggestion graciously...and she wasn't...no, she wasn't going to accept this emotional pressure graciously either!

She struggled in vain, tried desperately to escape his ruthless assault on her mouth, but he held her unnaturally firmly for a man with the use of just one arm.

His mouth shifted from her lips and grazed tantalisingly to her earlobe. 'Strong, aren't I?' he teased in her ear.

'Amazingly so. All brawn and no brain,' she hissed insultingly.

'I can outwit you every inch of the way, Justine,' he murmured seductively as he nibbled at her earlobe.

His hand still held her firmly in the small of her back. He seemed to have located a pressure point at the base of her spine that paralysed her. She couldn't move and, dear God, she didn't want to. She had begged for this moment from the first time she had ever set eyes on him and now it was really happening.

Her head cleared and she pulled back forcibly at the precise moment he eased the pressure from her back. She staggered and his hand snaked out and caught her wrist to steady her.

'I'm sure when you're sober you'll warm to the idea of driving me to Scotland.'

'And I'm sure when *you're* sober you'll wish tonight had never happened!'

'And I'm sure you're right but the regrets could be fun to reveal,' he mocked.

'No chance of that happening because I am not, positively not driving a one-armed bandit *anywhere*!'

He was still gripping her wrist, tightly, but his thumb caressed the back of her hand and that was far more painful. Tiny caresses that burned her skin.

'You are, dear Justine, because that is what I want——'

'And you always get what you want, don't you?' she seethed through tight pale lips.

'Will I get what I want from you?' His blue eyes widened in expectation; there was a mocking tilt to his lips and she guessed he wasn't referring to the drive.

Justine was stone-cold sober now. So this was the game, was it? Not very sportsmanlike, but he never had been fair. He'd probably been fouling when someone chukkaed him off his polo pony.

'No,' she stated defiantly. 'I've no intention of sleeping with you on those overnight stops you meaningfully suggested to my brother-in-law.'

Dark brows arched over those ice-blue eyes. 'Oh, so that's what's on your mind, is it?' He smiled slowly. 'Well, sorry to disappoint you, but I think you misinterpreted the whole suggestion.' He let go of her wrist to tap his strapped arm. 'I need a driver, Justine, not a lover.'

The colour rose to her face and she could do nothing to hide it from him. Clever move, Max Benedict, she fumed inside. So now you think you have the measure of me? Wrong.

She smiled sweetly, in control again, the fire gone from her face and directed to the remark that slid lethally from her lips to fall at his feet.

'So you kiss your other chauffeur like that, do you?'

There was a giveaway glint of metallic anger in his eyes, as if he didn't know how to take that, and then it was gone and as he threw his head back and laughed Richard stepped back into the room.

'So pleased to see you two getting on so well——'

'Like a house on fire!' Justine snapped and brushed past her brother-in-law to the hall where the air was much sweeter.

It was even sweeter in her bedroom and she slammed shut her door and breathed so deeply that the infusion to her lungs nearly overcame her.

Giving herself a mental and physical shake, she proceeded to strip off her violet dress, balled it and hurled it at the wall.

'Oh, I shouldn't have missed!' she wailed. 'I should have KOed you the last time we met, Max Benedict. And I won't, I just *won't* drive you anywhere!'

'You will, Justine! We insist on it!' Teresa told her sharply at breakfast the next morning.

Two against one. Justine glared at them both over the breakfast-table and then lowered her eyes to concentrate on scrubbing butter on her toast.

'He's an insufferable man and the idea of driving him all that way is absurd. I don't for a minute believe that he's afraid of flying. I bet there just isn't an airline that has a wide-bodied jet big enough to accommodate his massive ego!'

'What on earth have you got against the man?' Richard asked in surprise at her outburst.

'He spurned her years ago at a cocktail party, that's what she's got against him,' Teresa said spitefully, and Richard raised surprised brows.

And some more, Justine thought peevishly.

'He certainly didn't appear to be spurning you last night, Justine. He seemed very taken with you,' Richard tried to praise.

'He must have suffered a blow to his head as well as his arm, then,' Teresa said, pouring more coffee for her husband.

'Ha, ha, Teresa's made a funny,' Justine gibed sarcastically.

'That's enough, Justine. When are you going to grow up?' Richard reprimanded.

Justine slammed down her knife. She'd had enough, more than a human being could take.

'Why is it that whenever I open my voice to express an opinion it's always "that's enough, Justine"? What is it you've both got against me? Is it because I bucked the system? Went off round the world and did my own thing—something neither of you would ever have the guts to do!'

Teresa's eyes narrowed murderously. 'You absconded away from family responsibilities——'

'You made those responsibilities your own, Teresa. I'm not like you and I didn't want to go into the family business and don't blame me for your failings. You weren't such a great success yourself. If you hadn't married Richard——'

'That's enough, Justine——'

'Oh, my God,' sighed Justine in disbelief, snatching for the coffee-pot and pouring herself a cup. She couldn't win with these two, so why try?

'Don't forget your sister is pregnant and she doesn't need this upset,' Richard reminded her.

Emotional blackmail again!

'I was talking with your father last night on the phone,' Richard went on gravely. 'And things aren't looking good in Europe either. He hasn't had much success. Recycling is big and we don't——'

'And so it should be,' Justine cut in. 'All those trees being murdered so people can wrap their fish and chips. "That's enough, Justine",' she mimicked, and then let out a deep sigh as no one said a word. Yes, she was being childish—again. 'I know,' she went on, subdued now. 'Recycling has its limitations and that's why you don't use it. You end up with a fibrous mash after a while.' She looked across at her sister and brother-in-law, who were watching her intently. 'And it's not profitable. You just about break even.'

Richard raised the ubiquitous brow again. 'So you do know a bit about the business after all.'

'I know enough to know that Hammond's products are exceptionally good quality without the need to demolish the rainforests to get it. I also know that Daddy is on his last legs trying to drum up business and I don't want to be responsible... well, he's not as young as he was...'

'At last you're seeing a bit of sense,' Teresa said quickly. 'So you will drive Max Benedict to Scotland next week.'

It wasn't a question, simply a bald statement of fact. Justine had brooded on it most of the night. If it were anyone but Mega-Max she would do it willingly. She did want to help; she'd be some sort of a monster if she didn't want to in spite of all she said to the contrary. She cared deeply for her father and she didn't want to see him go under the way she had done so easily. She was young and could start again but for a middle-aged man to lose his lifetime's work... it went beyond comprehension.

'I want to help...' Justine started, toying with a piece of toast on her plate.

'You didn't want to last night, before and during the dinner party,' Teresa bit out. 'You behaved abominably——'

'That's just me,' Justine told her. 'You should know me by now, Teresa——'

'Don't let's start that all over again,' Richard said, glancing at his watch. 'I've got work to do. It's settled. You'll do it, Justine.'

Justine looked up at him as he stood from the table. 'What was your intention if he hadn't made that suggestion, Richard?'

'What exactly do you mean by that?' Teresa asked suspiciously.

'You said it last night, Teresa, something about me being the whole point, the cosy little foursome. Then you left us alone in the drawing-room for ages and we both got the impression it was all set up. I'd hate to think you were using me as bait.'

'That was never the intention,' Richard spluttered, going very red in the face, and Justine knew with a miserable certainty that it had been. 'The idea... yes, the idea was to have a pleasant evening together in the hope that Max would look favourably on the company and consider using us.'

'Which he is doing, without my interference. I told you, Teresa, Max doesn't work like that. He'll make up his own mind and you two trying to thrust me into his bed *en route* to the mill——'

'Justine!' Teresa exploded, going quite pale. 'We aren't asking anything of the sort! You go from bad to worse in your thinking.'

'I'm thinking about it very logically,' Justine reasoned. 'Max Benedict has a reputation and I'm hardly Quasimodo in drag. We're going to be stuck in a car together for hours on end and those overnight stops are inevitable and one thing could lead to another...'

She didn't have to say any more. Teresa shot to her feet. Any thoughts on sibling protection that Justine was striving to bring home to her sister crashed on to stony ground with Teresa's next words.

'Remember one thing, Justine, dear,' she grated heatedly. 'He didn't want you years ago at that party and nothing has changed. He even arrived last night with his mistress after leading Richard to believe he was interested...' Her voice trailed off as she realised what she was saying. Richard looked quite mortified and cleared his throat loudly.

'It wasn't quite like that, Teresa, darling——'

'I know just what it was like,' Justine mumbled and got to her feet and started to clear the plates. She carried a stack out towards the kitchen, kicking the breakfast-room door shut with the back of her heel, and then she paused, eavesdropping on the row that was exploding behind her as soon as she had vacated the room.

'This has all got out of hand, Teresa——'

'It was all your idea in the first place, after I told you the way he'd looked at her years ago——'

'And then you just said he'd spurned her. Make up your mind!'

'He did spurn her,' Teresa insisted. 'Probably because she was just a kid at the time, but not before he'd looked his fill. I just thought that four years later he might be more interested. And it was you who said he'd sounded interested on the phone when you mentioned her. Anyway, it's quite obvious now that he isn't because he brought his latest girlfriend with him——'

'I'd say he has a very deep interest,' Richard blustered. 'Why the suggestion from him that she drives him up there and not Beverley?'

'How the hell should I know?' Teresa stormed. 'Anyway, Justine's wrong in thinking he'd try anything on the way up to the mill. Max likes real women, like that lovely Beverley. Justine hasn't a chance; he's just using her for a bit of sport and flattering her ego by making that suggestion and we'll go along with it because we need that damned contract——'

Justine didn't hear any more. She slammed the breakfast dishes in the dishwasher, making a tremendous noise as she mumbled pitifully to herself. 'But you weren't here when he kissed me!' Then she slammed shut the door and set the machine in motion and leaned hopelessly against it as it gurgled merrily.

But Teresa had a point. Justine Hammond was just a bit of sport to the man. He had kissed her and a thousand others beside and that was his sport now that his polo days were obviously over. And wasn't she just being a teeny bit presumptuous in thinking he had seduction on his mind when he had denied it? Wishful thinking on her part, maybe? More than likely, but what was a certainty was that she would do her best for her father, and another certainty was that she wasn't going to allow Max Benedict to get to her. He was a tease, a menacing tease, and he had time on his hands waiting for the next operation and why not indulge himself in a bit of fun? So long as she kept that in mind she'd be OK.

Yes, she would flat-pack her emotions along with her overnight bag when the time came. Because she could handle Max Benedict all right—yes, she could!

CHAPTER FOUR

'TELEPHONE for you, Justine,' Janet called out as Justine came tripping down the stairs, rubbing her arms in a thick sweater.

'Is there any heating on, Janet? I'm freezing upstairs.'

'Cutbacks,' Janet told her grimly as she held her hand over the mouthpiece of the phone. 'I lit a fire for you in the sitting-room and the kitchen's warm. Miss Teresa said there's no point in keeping the heating running while they're away. Are you ready for your morning coffee yet?'

'Yes, please. I'll join you in the kitchen for it.' She took the telephone from her.

Cutbacks, eh? Well, as she wasn't in a monetary position to offer any housekeeping at the moment she supposed she shouldn't complain that Teresa was being frugal, though it was easy to be frugal when you weren't here suffering, Justine thought dejectedly. She'd have to get a job soon, very soon, and somewhere else to live.

'Hello.'

'Justine?'

Justine froze even more. 'Yes, who's that?' She knew very well who it was, though she had long since given up ever hearing from him again. And so had poor Richard and Teresa, hence a bored Teresa joining her husband on his business trip to Europe.

'The one-armed bandit. Are you ready?'

Her eyes went skywards. 'Ready for what?'

'This trip, of course. Scotland, isn't it?'

'I thought you'd gone off the idea. You said you'd make arrangements with Richard on Monday but you didn't. He's been going frantic these last few days waiting for your call. He's on his way to Brussels or somewhere now and taken a very dejected Teresa with him.'

'I don't bother with the monkey when it's the organ grinder I want,' he laughed.

Justine couldn't help a small smile creasing her face. 'Memory like an elephant, eh? How's the arm?'

'Agony, you'll be pleased to hear. The pain-killers are so hefty I'll probably be in a stupor most of the trip, so that should put your mind at ease.'

'I doubt I'll notice the difference,' she bit back sarcastically and poked her tongue out at the mouthpiece of the phone. 'So you're serious about this trip? I hope you have a doctor's note to say you're fit to travel.'

'No, but I've got one from Mummy to say she approves.'

'Well, I knew you didn't have a father,' she joked meaningfully, 'but a mummy comes as a bit of a surprise too. I thought you'd originated from a spore.'

She held the receiver away from her ear as he laughed.

'I can see this trip is going to whisk away my blues.'

Justine frowned. 'Are you depressed, then?'

'In the depths. I badly need cheering up. I can't work with this arm. I can't do any sport. I can't do anything.'

And why not pass the time by insisting on this futile trip to Scotland? Justine thought, unaccountably depressed.

'Sorry, but my heart doesn't bleed for you. If you play hard you get hurt hard.'

'And I repeat, you are some hard lady——'

'Not to be softened, so don't get any ideas around Huddersfield.'

'You're the one with all the novel ideas, sweetheart. So what time can you pick me up?'

Justine gasped. 'Just like that, eh? You expect me to drop everything when you whistle and come running?'

'Yup, I sure do. Have you got a pen handy?'

'Just a minute.' She scrabbled for a pen among the piles of letters on the hall table. 'OK, fire away.'

A few minutes later she put down the receiver, shaking now—and it wasn't too much to do with the sub-zero temperatures in the draught-ridden hall of the old manor. Everyone had given him up for good. Richard and Teresa had sunk into a no-hope gloom and had eventually gone off on their trip wondering what they were going to tell John Hammond when they met up with him in Brussels. The temptation to phone them and tell them Max was going ahead with the trip was curbed. There were no guarantees that Max would give Hammond the contract, not until he had seen over the mill at least, and then? Justine didn't know. All she knew, all she could reasonably recognise at the moment, was that she was going to act as Max's chauffeur for a few days. It was going to happen, she was going to drive Max Benedict up to Scotland... Heavens! A new thought struck her: she was going to have to drive him back as well! In all it would take a better part of a week. A whole week with that man! Did she fully realise what she was letting herself in for?

She hugged herself tightly as she made her way to the kitchen for her coffee. That light-hearted phone call was aeons away from what had been troubling her since the dinner party. Her head still throbbed with the effort of coldly dismissing the effect that wretched kiss had had on her senses.

Time and time again she had tried to convince herself, though it hurt to do so, that Teresa was right: Max Benedict liked real women and she didn't stand a ghost of a chance with him. Well, she knew that already. He'd made it painfully obvious twice before. How many more times did she need it rammed home to her? Trouble was, she couldn't separate two issues here. She was doing this with a purpose, to help get this contract for the family business, but personal issues seemed to be taking centre stage. If he hadn't kissed her that way she might have been able to concentrate on what this was all about but Max had personalised the whole thing with that assault on her senses. Games? She could play too, but she wasn't at all sure what the rules were yet.

So what attitude should she take on this trip to save her soul from the devil himself, Max Benedict? The light-hearted approach like their telephone call? The aloof approach, the vulnerable approach, the sophisticated approach? Oh, hell, none of them sat easily on the shoulders of her personality apart from the first one. Well, that was settled, then. She'd be *herself* and to blazes with him.

She stopped at the kitchen door and paused to rub her forehead fiercely. To be true to yourself you had to know yourself, and what Justine knew was that, though she had tried to convince herself, and her sister, that she didn't even like the man, the truth was that she did like him—rather a lot.

'Oh, I need this coffee, Janet,' she buzzed as she stepped into the warm welcoming kitchen. 'Hot, sweet and satisfyingly milky, because I fear I'm in for a bumpy ride over the next few days.'

'I don't like motorways,' Max admitted as they pored over the road map in the sumptuous drawing-room of his Ascot home later that day. 'They're a bore.'

When he'd given her his address over the phone she'd been surprised he lived in the same county, presuming he lived in the heart of London and secretly dreading the struggle through the city's traffic congestion. She'd taken Teresa's car without a qualm, a comfortable Volvo which should withstand the long journey without a problem, but Max had soon quashed that idea as soon as she'd arrived. It was his automatic Jaguar or nothing and now he was being picky about the route she was proposing to take.

'You don't like flying, rail travel, or motorways.' Justine sighed in exasperation. 'What do you like, Max Benedict?'

'I like the perfume you're wearing,' he murmured appreciatively as he leaned closer to her.

Justine shifted away from him and started jotting in her pad, taking note of alternative routes and inwardly agreeing that motorway travel was boring. But they were the quickest route from A to B and the least time spent with him, the safer all round. 'You're not taking this seriously, are you?' she murmured.

'And you are?' he said, moving in on her again to look over her shoulder at the alternative road numbers she was jotting down.

Justine straightened up and glared at him. 'Yes, I am. You want a driver and you've got one, a reluctant one at that. I don't want to do this but I'm doing it because Hammond's wants your wretched contract. Not that I think me driving you anywhere but round the bend will make one iota of difference, but I'm simply indulging the whim of a spoilt, rich, one-armed client who enjoys playing games because frankly I've nothing better to do with my time *and* if I don't do it I'll never be able to face my family again.'

He gave her a thin smile. 'Does that matter? From what I've seen there's not much love lost between all of you.'

Justine stiffened. 'Families stick together——'

'No one stuck to you that night of the dinner party. You were treated with positive derision.'

Justine bowed her head over the road map again. 'I've always been treated that way by my sister,' she mumbled.

'Jealousy?'

She looked up into his eyes again and frowned and murmured, 'I don't think so.' Frankly she'd not given it much thought before, just assumed that all sisters rowed. 'Jealous of what?' she added after a second of ponderous thought.

'You're much more beautiful than her, for one thing,' he suggested, a teasing glint in his eye.

Justine's eyes widened in surprise. 'I don't think that has anything to do with anything.'

Max shrugged. 'Maybe she's jealous of your freedom, then. You've travelled a lot.'

Justine smiled and shook her head. 'Teresa isn't a traveller. She would never have dared do the things I've done. I bucked the system; that's the root of our disagreements, I suppose. Our mother left when I was a tot and although Teresa's only seven years older than me she felt responsible for me and my father, but I wouldn't conform and that must have irritated her.'

'And you still don't conform?'

'I'm not like Teresa, willing to live under my father's roof in exchange for being mistress of the house. I wanted my independence as soon as I came out of college. I wanted to be a photographer and I wanted to travel. I followed my heart whereas she followed what she thought were her duties.' She shrugged. 'I don't think for a minute she envies me my independence, because I haven't any any more. I'm the failure; she's the one sitting pretty with her husband and a baby on the way.'

'Do you envy her that?' Max countered, quite seriously, which made Justine laugh.

'What—a husband and a baby on the way?' she asked incredulously.

'It's what a lot of young women yearn for.'

Justine grinned. 'Not this young woman,' she told him decisively. 'Once I've recovered from this setback I'll pick myself up, brush myself down and start all over again. And I think we'd better make a start now before it gets dark.' She started to fold up the map, aware that he was still gazing at her. She wished he wouldn't do that, study her so intently, it made her spine tingle.

'Hell, it wasn't Munich, was it?' Justine's spine was stiff now and Max's eyes were glittering with humour. 'It was Belgravia. The launch of one of my magazines. You cornered me——'

'I've never been to Belgravia in my life,' Justine retorted, lying through her teeth but making her voice sound as if it wasn't. 'Now are we going, or aren't we?'

Grinning now, Max reached for her pad and stripped off the page she had scribbled laboriously on. He crumpled it in his good hand and tossed it into the fireplace. 'We don't need that. Let's play it by ear. Go where our instincts take us. First stop the Launceston Hotel just outside Bath. I've booked a suite there for the night——'

'Just a minute!' Justine protested hotly. The whole of her insides were aflame. Damn him! Total recall. He'd remembered.

'Just a minute what?' he urged. And yes, there was a gleam of knowing in his eyes and another one of gentle mockery. He was going to make a meal of this on their travels. Justine felt it in her bones. Teenage starry-eyed adoration? He'd known. Four years ago he hadn't the time and the inclination to take advantage of it . . . Oh, God, he had time on his hands now, well one of them at least, she thought with near hysteria. As for the inclination, well, he had kissed her that way, which showed he had the inclination now all right . . . and just now hadn't she laid scorn on husbands and babies, claiming it wasn't for her? Dear God, the man probably though he was home and dry. No commitment but a bit of sport with someone with no ties or permanent aspirations in mind who had gazed at him so adoringly a lifetime ago.

'Bath!' she almost screeched. 'That doesn't sound like playing it by ear. You've already booked a suite and besides it's miles off the route to Scotland,' she protested.

'Is it, now?' he drawled mockingly. 'It's a beautiful place, though, a place I've longed to revisit since my childhood——'

'You never had a childhood! Spores don't have a childhood!' she insulted bitingly. 'And this isn't a Cook's world tour, you know——'

His eyes darkened. 'This trip is going to be whatever I wish it to be, Justine. Remember that,' he grated menacingly. 'You might be in the driving seat but metaphorically I am.'

'In other words take it or leave it?' she hissed.

The menace was still there in his tone but there was a definite gleam of mockery in his eyes. 'Enjoy it, Justine. Just relax and enjoy it.' He tapped his bad arm with his good hand. 'Most women would give their right arm to be in your sweet little driving shoes.'

'My God!' Justine breathed in disbelief. 'Your lack of modesty is something else, Max Benedict. I'll tell you one thing before we leave. You're taking your life in that one good hand of yours, expecting me to play your games on this trip. I can be as unsportsmanlike as you when I choose.'

'And don't I know it?' he teased, warming now. 'And I'll tell *you* one thing before we leave. We go where I want to go because I have every intention of enjoying this trip——'

Her eyes narrowed dangerously. 'You're not even vaguely interested in the mill, are you?'

'Oh, yes, I am, and don't you forget it, Justine. It's the whole point of this trip, after all, but there's nothing to stop us having fun on the way. Don't spoil it. You fail me, sweetheart, and I'll fail your family business.'

'That's blackmail!' she cried, aghast at his nerve.

'Emotional blackmail,' he corrected. 'I told you I'm not above it.'

'And you're not above trying to seduce me *en route*, either, are you?'

He raised a sardonic brow. 'Why do you persist on that line of thinking? It's almost as if you're willing it to happen.'

'I'm not willing for anything to happen between us on this trip, Max. But one thing about you has made me very wary. You kissed me the other night——'

'What's a kiss between friends?' he interjected teasingly. His hand came up and touched her chin, his thumb caressing the edge of her lower lip as if he was about to give her another of his *friendly* kisses.

Justine stepped back, out of his reach. Her tongue snaked out to whisk away the heat of that touch from her lip. 'But we aren't friends, Max Benedict, and it wasn't that sort of kiss. It was the full-blown thing. The sort of kiss that is the fore-runner to something else...'

How could she go on when he was looking at her this way, his eyes teasing hers, not taking it at all seriously? And that kiss had been serious and what could happen if he took it a step further would be serious.

'Well . . . well, say something, then!' she blurted.

He shrugged and smiled thinly. 'What on earth can I say to that?'

'Deny it, for one thing!' Oh, please do. Say you were drunk or something? That you hadn't meant to, it was just a slip of the tongue!

'How can I deny something that happened so positively? I kissed you, you were there.'

Justine sighed in exasperation. 'I want you to deny that it was a forerunner to something else. When a man kisses a woman it's always, but always, for a reason. You just don't go around kissing people that way for nothing.'

'Sometimes the urge comes for no reason, though. An impulse, a whim, a feeling——'

'No, a reason,' Justine insisted. She wasn't going to let him get out of it, try as he might. She knew she was being wound up like a clockwork mouse for the cat's fun but she wasn't in the mood for fun. She was going to spend a lot of time with this man and she wanted to make everything clear before they set off. 'Max Benedict doesn't do things on impulse or a whim.'

'How do you know that?'

'I . . . I don't,' she floundered. What did she know about the man? Next to nothing. He was rich enough, powerful enough, seductive enough to get away with whimsy. 'Is . . . is all this a game to you?' she went on bravely. 'This whole trip up to

Scotland? You . . . you say you can't play any sport, or work or do anything with your bad arm so . . . so are you just whiling away your time until your next operation?'

He laughed then and shook his head as if he couldn't believe what she had just said. 'We're going to Scotland because I want to see over your father's mill. I have a very valuable contract that I review every year and——'

'Yes, yes. I know all that,' she sighed. 'But that's not the issue. I mean . . . I . . .'

'What do you mean, Justine?' he asked quietly, just a hint of mockery left now.

She looked at him then, really looked at him. He stood in front of her, so tall and daunting and so self-composed that she felt small and insignificant in his presence. She also felt that if she carried on this conversation she might hear something that she didn't want to. Wasn't she just trying to push him into admitting that that kiss was something special? My God, hadn't her travels in strange parts better equipped her with some modicum of maturity? Obviously not, because she didn't know how to handle this man though she had thought she could. Yes, what was a kiss? She was trying to make an issue out of nothing.

'I think we'd better get a move on,' she stated flatly, reaching for the map and bending to pick up her bag from the floor. 'Bath calls, and then where, Max, Carlisle via the Isle of Wight?'

'I've never been to the Isle of Wight,' he said thoughtfully as they left the room.

'Well, don't get any ideas,' she warned as Max picked up a holdall and struggled with a suit bag in the hall. 'I've no intention of indulging more of your whims than is necessary on this trip. We'll take in Bath because I'd like to see it too...I'll take that.' She took the suit bag from him and draped it over her arm and tried to take the holdall from him as well.

'I can manage this,' he told her abruptly. 'I'm not totally incapacitated.'

'Early days yet,' she threw over her shoulder as she ran down the steps to load up the car, and she heard Max laugh softly behind her.

'Isn't that just my luck?' Max breathed despondently, peering out of the windscreen as they swished into the car park of the hotel.

Justine shifted the gear lever into park, pulled up the handbrake and switched off the ignition. 'Isn't what just your luck?' She peered too, wondering what he was trying to look at through the mist of rain that covered the windscreen.

'Rain and mist to cloud the spectacle of Bath lit at night. It's out there somewhere. They say it's magical.'

'Well, if we'd come via the motorway as I suggested we'd have been here sooner.'

'And if we'd been here sooner it would have defeated the object of seeing Bath by night. It's pouring anyway, whatever the time of day.'

She grinned. 'It's a dumb time of the year to see the sights anyway.'

'Trouble with you is you have no romance in your soul, Justine Hammond,' he said as he got out of the car.

'Romance? Where does that come in? It's teeming down, freezing cold and I'm starving—nothing romantic in that!' She went round to the boot, pulling the cowl neck of her sweater up round her neck. His hand was on her elbow before she could heave it open.

'They have porters for that,' he told her, and hurried her to the hotel steps.

'You sound like my sister,' she said under her breath as they stepped into the foyer.

The suite was warm and welcoming and Justine bent her head and shook the raindrops from her hair as Max tipped the porter and closed the door after him. He came towards her, soundless on the thick carpet so she jumped when his hand came up to fold down the neck of her sweater. Her eyes were bright and startled as they met his.

'You know you never breathed a word of objection when I told you I'd booked a suite for us here,' he said with a small smile on his lips.

'There wasn't any point, because I don't object.'

'I thought you would.'

That was exactly why she hadn't made an issue of it. He'd been baiting her when he'd said it, had expected an explosion. Well, he'd soon find out that she did little of what was expected of her.

'You thought wrong, then. I see nothing untoward in a couple sharing a suite, especially when they only have three arms between them.' She smiled sweetly at him. 'You'll need help and anything Beverley can do I can do better—the difference being that I don't hunger for your body as she does.'

His eyes were bright with mischief. 'But I might hunger for yours in the middle of the night.'

Justine was getting used to his way of teasing her. He treated her as if she were still that adoring teenager who had accosted him years ago. She felt quite safe with it but at the same time she couldn't help feeling an occasional shower of disappointment that he was treating all this as if it was a huge joke.

'Room Service can satisfy any hungers you might suffer in the night,' she told him bluntly.

He smiled and lifted his hand to brush a droplet of water she had missed from her brow. 'I hope by the time we get to Scotland some of that biting charm of yours has softened.'

Justine steeled herself then. She could feel it softening now as he gazed down at her, his own hair wet and dishevelled by that short spurt in the elements to get to the hotel from the car park. She too wanted to raise her hand to his brow and brush away the droplets, but that would be a small gesture of submission and she mustn't submit to this man, because a price would have to be paid for her weakness and she couldn't afford him.

Without a word she turned away and went to her bags. She'd already noticed that there were two bedrooms to the suite, not that she had expected there not to be. Max Benedict was a tease but not even he would be so outrageously pushy as to have booked only one bedroom on their first night together.

'I'm going to take a bath,' she told him from the doorway of one of the bedrooms. 'I expect you want one too. Can you manage to undress on your own?'

'And if I can't?' He held her eyes, daring her.

She didn't know. She didn't know if she could do that for him. She felt heat rise to her face at the thought and then she saw him smile and knew that he had seen her uncertainty. But he didn't push it, and somehow that was worse than if he had made some inane remark.

'W-what about eating?' she asked in a small voice, still poised in the doorway of the bedroom.

His left arm moved across to his right and ran lightly over it. She'd noticed him doing that in the car on the way. He didn't seem to know he was doing it and Justine supposed it was an involuntary gesture brought about by the constant ache.

'Actually I'd rather eat in the suite,' she added quickly. She didn't think for a minute he was self-conscious about his disability, but he looked tired and she was tired too and she really couldn't trust herself not to spill something down him again in public.

'I'm easy,' he said. 'I'll order while you bathe. Any preferences?'

'Anything. I'm so hungry I could eat a poached duvet.'

He was still smiling when she closed the door on him as he picked up the phone.

Justine bathed quickly, not allowing herself the luxury of dozing off in the heavenly warmth that silked around her. She wondered how he coped with undressing and bathing and dressing again with that crooked arm of his. She held her right arm stiffly against her chest when she got out of the bath, to see what it was like. She struggled to dry herself, to moisturise her body, to slide herself into her robe, all with one hand. Heavens, it was such a struggle. She didn't give up, though. She combed through her wet hair and tried to blow dry it with her left hand. It was nearly impossible. It took an age to dress. She'd never realised how useful two arms were. She couldn't do up her bra, that *was* impossible. At least he didn't wear one, but he wore pants surely? She struggled with hers and managed but she was hot with impatience by the time she'd eased her bikini briefs over her narrow hips. Leggings too were awkward and when she stood up they were horribly twisted round her calves. Tights or stockings would be impossible! He wore none of these but nevertheless she sympathised.

After struggling to pull a sweater over her head she was so exhausted she slumped down on the edge of the bed and breathed deeply. Both her arms were aching pitifully. However did he manage to button up a shirt? It was then the full reality of his disability hit her. Yes, it was a temporary disability, but supposing the next operation wasn't successful... Her heart ached for him. On impulse she went to his bedroom and without knocking opened the door and stopped dead at the sight of him.

He was sprawled on the bed, propped up against the headboard, freshly laundered and dressed in black cords and a dark green silk shirt. The phone at his ear was held in place by his shrugged shoulder and with his left hand he was taking notes, jotting expertly and 'hmm'ing down the phone.

Justine stood in the doorway with her mouth gaping open. His shirt-sleeves were rolled back and the vivid blue and purple scar was clearly visible across his right elbow and down his forearm. It was an appalling scar, livid and deep, but once over the initial shock she let that ache of sympathy for him seep away from her. She had actually felt sorry for him—had rushed in here to offer him her help but it was quite apparent he didn't need it!

'Yes, sweetheart, I've got it,' he murmured down the phone. 'Yes, I'll call you tomorrow. It's not a problem.' He put the phone back in its cradle, picked up his pen and scribbled some more and then he looked across to her.

'Enjoy your bath?'

'Enjoy my bath?' she echoed sarcastically, so inflamed that she was threatened with internal combustion. 'No, I didn't! It was a nightmare because I took your advice and tried it one-handed, to see how awful it must be for you without the use of your right arm, but I needn't have bothered because you...*you* are left-handed!'

He looked at her as if she were half demented, slid his legs over the side of the bed and stood up, grinning, damn him! Grinning like a Cheshire cat!

'Ambidextrous, actually,' he told her with a degree of pride. 'And very useful it is too.' He proceeded to adjust the leather strap across his bad arm and Justine wanted to adjust it round his neck!

'I felt sorry for you!' she blurted.

'Nice to know you care,' he muttered, but she thought she detected a thread of disapproval of what she had just admitted.

'Don't be so damned facetious,' she spluttered on. 'I struggled in the bath, struggled dressing, realised how awkward it must be for you, and what do I find when I come in here to help you... I find you showered and dressed and chatting merrily to...to...who was it—Bev? Or is she history now?' She waved her hand dismissively, not giving him a chance to answer. 'Whoever...someone close enough to be called sweetheart anyway...and writing...writing expertly with your rotten left hand...'

'Justine——'

'Don't *Justine* me!' she flamed on. 'I don't like being taken for a ride, metaphorically or otherwise——'

She could get no more of her fury out because suddenly he was upon her and that very *expert* left hand of his had circled her waist and had scooped her so close up against him that her eyes could scarcely focus on his face.

'This is all very interesting,' he breathed dangerously, tightening his grip around her till she could hardly breathe. 'What am I supposed to make of it all?'

'What are you getting at?' she croaked back but she knew, oh, yes, she knew and what a fool she had been to leave herself wide open to this.

'You come rushing in here without knocking, find me talking to someone on the phone——'

'Not a someone, a sweetheart!' Justine rallied, past caring now. 'And yes, I do object to that, because she could be driving you to Scotland instead of me. *She* could be feeling sorry for you, not me. And I am not jealous, no, I am not!'

He looked down at her and she expected to see those clear blue eyes sparkling with triumph, that tantalising mouth creasing at the corners with mockery because she had given herself away. Instead she saw the glint of anger as those eyes darkened, the uncompromising thinning of his lips.

'I don't recall mentioning jealousy, Justine,' he said quietly, straining to hold on to his temper.

Of course he hadn't, but she knew that was what he had been hinting at and her very denial of it was condemning enough. But she had expected some sort of triumph to overcome him at her giveaway denial; instead he was stiff with anger against her.

'It...it was...it was what you were thinking, though,' she tried bravely.

'It was indeed, but jealousy isn't the issue here.' His arm tightened even more viciously around her waist. His voice was harsh when he went on, 'Don't pity me, Justine. I can't take pity so don't waste it on me. When I make love to you, you give yourself because you can't deny yourself, *not*, and I repeat, *not* because you feel sorry for me. Have I made myself clear?'

Justine was speechless. She parted her lips to try and utter some sort of blatant put-down about ditchwater but the words just wouldn't come. She supposed he saw her stricken dumbness as some sort of answer, because when his lips came down to hers they weren't issuing another warning...more a soft acceptance of her acceptance of his terms.

Jealousy? It was nothing, not an issue, as he had said. Desire was, though; it throbbed deep inside and had nothing to do with feeling sorry for this man. And denial, that too was an issue. Could she deny herself? She didn't know that yet but it was a heady warning and that was all that was clear.

CHAPTER FIVE

JUSTINE finally broke away from him, deeply ashamed of herself for taking so long about it. But time had stood still as that kiss had gone on and on, dragging her emotions backwards and sideways.

But it was only a kiss—another. He'd made no attempt to add anything more, to take it a step further.

'I suppose that was another test,' she muttered bitterly as she stepped back from him and pulling at his arm to release it from the small of her back.

'A test to see if you are willing?' His tone was soft and lilting. A tease again. He let her tug at his arm and then dropped it to his side.

'Well, wasn't it?'

She didn't wait for a reply but walked out of the bedroom and over to the window of the main room. She pulled back the curtains because it was something to do rather than face him and this treacherous feeling inside her. He hadn't wasted any time in making yet another pass at her and that was bad news, but what was worse was that she had practically asked for it. Why hadn't she left well alone instead of making a fuss about his very capable left hand and the jealousy thing? She was jealous, damn it, madly jealous of 'sweetheart', and she shouldn't be and she wasn't going to show any more weakness because she had a life to lead after all this and Max Benedict wouldn't be a part of it.

The rain had ceased, the mist had cleared and the beautiful town of Bath in the distance was indeed a magical sight with its twinkling street-lights picking out the magnificent crescents.

'Your dream has come true,' she told him, aware of him stepping into the room to join her.

She heard the clatter of a salver and then his soft laughter. 'And so has yours. Poached duvet, wasn't it?'

She turned then and he was standing by a trolley and peering down at something he had just uncovered. 'Or is it poached salmon?'

'Poached whatever, I'm going to eat it. What are you having?'

'The same.'

'You won't need my help, then, will you?' she told him with satisfaction, seating herself at the table and proceeding to dish up for them both. 'This just breaks up and yes,' she took a mouthful and closed her eyes in ecstasy, 'it just melts in the mouth.'

She opened her eyes to catch him watching her thoughtfully from across the other side of the table. 'What's wrong? Lost your appetite?' she said flippantly.

As soon as she said it she wished she hadn't. She realised he had no appetite and he was holding his arm again though she was sure he wasn't aware of it.

He's in pain, Justine thought miserably. She didn't want him to be in pain. His pain was her pain. But why take it on? she asked herself, and knew straight away. She cared, she really did, and that was dangerous, even more dangerous than the jealousy thing.

'It's delicious,' she told him. 'Try it while I open the wine.'

She struggled with the cork and finally it gave and she poured two glasses, wondering if he had taken his painkillers. The two didn't mix but she supposed he knew that.

He took the glass she offered, sampled it and then put it down and picked up his fork to eat.

'"Sweetheart" is my secretary,' he volunteered after a while.

He always seemed to be taking her unawares. There she was thinking he was suffering in silence and all he was doing was thinking of excuses to come up with to fool her. Secretary, my foot.

'"Sweetheart" as in Pussy Galore sort of thing? One of those fictional names writers come up with to grab our attention?'

He smiled and sipped more wine. 'Her real name is Lorna and "sweetheart" is a term of endearment I use for people I'm rather fond of.'

He'd called her 'sweetheart' as well, but the way it slid off his tongue it had sounded more like syrupy sarcasm.

Justine shrugged and helped herself to more salmon. 'So you're fond of her. Nothing unusual in that.'

'I didn't say there was but I don't want you to think there's anything more to it than fondness.'

'It doesn't matter to me what you do in your life. If you're bedding your secretary it has nothing to do with me.'

'But it has if I'm bedding you at the same time.'

Justine gulped her wine. 'But you're not bedding me,' she protested, her eyes wide with indignation.

'And I'm not bedding my secretary.'

'So you're not bedding either of us—what's that supposed to mean?'

He looked at her directly, full on, defying her not to meet his gaze, and when he answered his voice was deep and resonant. 'It means that I want you, Justine, and I don't want you to think I'm involved with anyone else. That wouldn't be fair.'

Fair? Nothing was fair in his nocturnal life.

She eyed him warily, determined to act with maturity because this was a very adult sort of a conversation, one that demanded honesty along with its forthrightness. She put down her knife and fork and picked up her wine glass and leaned back in her seat.

'So what would you call fair?' she quizzed rhetorically. 'Taking me to bed somewhere during this trip, me thinking that I *have* to do it otherwise you won't give my father your contract? I don't call emotional blackmail fair at all, Max.'

'The emotional blackmail came in the form of me getting you to come on this trip in the first place. The opportunity arose and I took full advantage of it. What we're talking about now is something quite different.'

'Well, I can't quite differentiate between the two, you see.'

'Well, you should try. I want to make love to you and I think you want it too——'

'OK, I won't make a prissy remark like...like... "don't kid yourself" ...because I'm tired of all these games. So you've admitted you want me and

I find you very attractive in spite of what you are putting me through and it would be very easy to do what you suggest but——'

'But you don't want to get involved,' he finished for her.

Justine attacked her wine as if it were the last glass in the world. She drained it in one and then with great reserve she placed the empty glass carefully down on the table. Oh, yes, she did want to get involved. That was the trouble. If she gave her heart to this man she would be too deeply involved ever to escape the pain of it. And it would cause her pain because he was just passing the time with her, playing his games of kiss-chase and never to be seen on her horizon again.

Suddenly he got up. 'Would you like to go into Bath for what's left of the evening?'

'Because you need a driver?'

His eyes narrowed. 'No, not because I need a driver. I just think it would be a nice thing for us to do while we're here. We'll take a taxi.'

She shook her head. She wanted to go but . . . she couldn't. 'I'd rather get some rest, but don't let me stop you.'

'You won't,' he said quietly, and it was obvious what he meant. He came round the table and bent and kissed her lightly on the forehead. 'Get your rest. Chester tomorrow for lunch, weather permitting.'

'Chester tomorrow for tea if we avoid the motorways,' she bit back as he went into his bedroom for his jacket.

At least Chester was north and on the way to Scotland. Why was he dragging it out like this? If she put her foot down she could make the whole journey tomorrow, weather permitting!

The weather. She watched the forecast on the television after he'd left. It didn't look good, more rain then a colder front coming in from the north. There was already snow in the Hebrides. Justine shivered and switched off the set. This really was a bad time of the year to be playing at Cook's tours—and to be playing Max-Benedict-type games.

She took herself off to bed with a slight headache and another ache somewhere in the region of her heart.

'Oh, it's quite incredible!' Justine enthused at the beautiful Tudor buildings and the galleried walkways above the shops in Chester. 'I could shop to death here.'

'You're supposed to be admiring the architecture, not the shops,' Max laughed as he edged her through the crowds of shoppers.

They had arrived around tea-time, as Justine had predicted, and there was a reservation for them at the Grosvenor, two de luxe double rooms which they were lucky to get—due to a cancellation according to Max—as Chester was jam-packed with Christmas shoppers.

And it was easy to understand why. The place was dripping with fabulous Christmas decorations and the whole city seemed to be buzzing. It was a late-night shopping day and the lights and the atmosphere were heady. Recession? It wasn't apparent here. There were street entertainers in the shopping precincts, buskers and acrobats, shops heaving with goods brightly displayed. Justine loved it all. She was even being nice to Max and that was because he was being nice to her. They hadn't argued once on the drive up, and when they had arrived at the hotel in the centre of town she was pleasantly warmed by the fact that he had booked *two* double rooms and not just the one. Only pleasantly warmed, though. She still didn't trust him.

'I bet there's a patron saint of shoppers in this city,' Justine laughed as they paused to admire the windows of a particularly fantastic jeweller's.

'There is,' Max informed her, frowning at the cost of a very remarkable diamond ring on a velvet cushion. 'St Cedryche; he was stoned to death at the city walls for asking outlandish prices for his jewellery and then declared a saint for making a hefty profit,' he told her with irony.

'You're kidding?' she breathed, staring at the gorgeous ring in awe and wondering where he had gleaned that bit of information from. She'd seen nothing of that in the guide book in the hotel.

'Yes, I was actually,' he grinned. 'I just made it up because St Michael was a bit obvious.'

She nearly punched his arm for that but she was on the wrong side of him and she'd noticed how he drew his bad arm across himself to protect it when the crowds of milling shoppers got too close.

'Shall we go back to the hotel now?' she asked, purposely making her voice sound weary. She wasn't a bit tired but she guessed the cold and the buzz of the shoppers was getting to him.

'Good idea. I've some calls to make.'

To 'sweetheart'? she wondered, feeling that odd pull at her heartstrings again.

They were still tugging hopelessly when he left her outside her room, suggesting they dined in the restaurant later and giving her a time to be ready.

She thought about him all the time she was getting ready. Fortunately the violet silk dress travelled well and fortunately she'd brought it with her! She'd anticipated that those overnight stops he'd suggested would hardly be taken in some dreary bed-and-breakfast establishments. Max lived well, travelled well; in fact he did everything in his life well. She wondered if he loved well too. So surely a man like him wouldn't be having an affair with his secretary?

She brushed out her luxurious dark Titian hair when she was dressed and decided she believed his denial that he wasn't having an affair with her. But he was probably having an affair with *someone*.

'And you're just light relief,' she decided as she went downstairs to join him. 'And a chauffeur and a helper at mealtimes, just like Beverley, who's history now, and one day you'll be history too, so remember all that and you'll be OK.'

'First sign of madness, talking to yourself,' he said softly behind her, joining her on the last sweep of stairs.

She smiled at him, knowing he couldn't have heard *exactly* what she had been mumbling to herself. 'It's when you get replies that you're in trouble,' she joked, and relished the warmth of his hand on her elbow as they walked into the opulent restaurant.

She relished the looks she was getting from the other diners as they ate as well, particularly from the female contingent. Max was probably right:

most women would give their right arm to be doing what she was doing, helping this charismatic man with one arm strapped to his chest.

'Don't overdo it, Justine,' he murmured once when she was being particularly overzealous. 'Remember I'm ambidextrous.'

'Don't spoil my fun,' she told him lightly, handing him back his fork. 'I don't expect I'll ever get the chance of having you practically eating out of my hand once you get the use of that arm back.'

'I must have brought the mother instinct out in you, then,' he laughed softly.

But it wasn't the mother instinct that kept her awake later, more the lover instinct. Much to her dismay she was enjoying this trip and she was enjoying Max Benedict too, and Scotland and the mill were a million miles away.

'Oh, this is ridiculous,' Justine fumed, reaching forward to rub the inside of the windscreen with the back of her hand.

Max leaned forward and impatiently flicked a switch. 'You've been driving this car long enough to know how to operate the de-mister, Justine.'

'I'm too busy looking out for signposts,' Justine gritted back. 'I hope you realise that this wretched tour of yours is beginning to be a pain in the butt.'

'I thought you were enjoying it,' he said tightly.

She had been but she wasn't going to admit it. They had left Chester early enough to get to York for lunch then spent a delightful hour or so wandering the beautiful city. He was great fun to be with and a fount of knowledge and she was enjoying it but now it was all going badly wrong and nerves were frayed.

Newcastle-upon-Tyne by the main highway by the evening was well within their scope but not if your 'back-seat driver' insisted on the scenic route through lonely bleak narrow roads across the moors with flurries of snow pestering the visibility. It was dark and they were hopelessly lost and it was all his fault.

'You took a wrong turning back there,' Max told her, studying the map on his lap.

Prickles of anger spurred her retort. 'Oh, well, of course it would be my fault, wouldn't it? Nothing to do with your unreasonable request to see the moors which you can't see anyway for the dark and the appalling weather. And put that light out. I can't see for looking!'

'OK, stop!'

Justine ignored him and pressed harder on the accelerator.

'Stop this minute before you have us in a ditch!' he grated harshly.

Justine came to a slithery stop in the middle of the road. She could see nothing ahead but a bank of whiteness, nothing behind but a bank of whiteness and she prayed that a juggernaut didn't appear out of nowhere though that was unlikely in a wilderness such as this.

'Get out,' he ordered.

'Get out? What for, to admire the view?' she bit out sarcastically.

'No, I'll drive from now on,' was the shocking retort.

Her breath caught in her throat at the very suggestion. 'Don't be ridiculous! You can't drive with one arm.'

'With one arm I'll make a better job of it than you are with two!' he rasped angrily.

Already he was half out of the door ready to come round to the driver's seat. He was furious and Justine knew it. She reached across and grabbed at his sweater, causing him to fall back into the passenger seat. In the dim interior light she saw the small wince of pain on his face and guilt swamped her.

'I... I'm all right,' she told him, picking up the map from the floor where it had slid as he'd tried to get out. 'We'll go on,' she added quietly, 'and stop at the next village for directions.'

'We'll stop at wherever you see a glimmer of light. There must be thousands of cottages out here,' he told her brusquely.

Tight-lipped, Justine drove on, her hands clenched around the steering-wheel. She could scarcely see the road in front of her and the white line down the centre of the road was fast being obliterated by the settling snow.

'Stop,' he ordered after a traumatic ten minutes when Justine thought they must be driving to the end of the world. Snow was building up on the windscreen and the wipers were struggling to clear it. 'Back up, slowly. I'll tell you when to stop.'

'How can I back up when I can't see a thing behind me?'

Max unbuckled his seatbelt and twisted round and brought his left arm across to grab at the steering-wheel. 'Put the car into reverse.'

Swallowing her anger and sudden nervousness Justine did as she was told and gingerly Max, with one hand, steered the car back along the tracks they had just made in the snow.

'Did you see lights?' She supposed viewing out of the side window you could see better than if looking ahead against a blanket of snow hitting the windscreen.

'No lights, but a farm gate. Farm gates usually lead to farms.'

There was a hint of sarcasm to that which made Justine think he was ruing the day he'd suggested this trip.

'OK, stop. There it is. Swing over. I'll get out and open it.'

Justine watched as he got out and shoulders hunched against the biting cold and the wind that was swirling the snow around his head he slithered to the five-bar gate, fumbled with the catch and swung it open. Slowly Justine drove through the gates and waited for him, her heart beating wildly at the thought of the struggle he must have had to get that huge gate open with one arm.

'I don't see any lights,' Justine murmured as, warily, she steered the car down a snowy track. She felt the solidness of concrete beneath the snow so she thought it must lead to somewhere but there was certainly no welcoming light anywhere in sight.

'There, to the right,' Max directed, and Justine steered the car through an archway and pulled up in front of a stone-built cottage. She heaved a sigh of relief but her nerves were still jangling as she registered that there wasn't a sign of life in the tiny remote cottage.

'There's no one here,' she said, but Max didn't hear because he was out of the car and already up the garden path. Justine left the car lights on so that he could see and got out herself, stuffing her hands up the sleeves of her sweater as she ran to join him in the porch of the cottage, shivering with cold and nerves.

Brushing the snow from her hair, she repeated, 'There's no one here.' Suddenly she was afraid because if there was no one here she would have to try and turn the car round in this tiny garden and anything could happen. They were hopelessly lost somewhere on the dangerous moors and they could slither into a ditch . . . be forced to spend the night in the car till daybreak . . . they would freeze . . . no one would find them.

'It's a holiday cottage,' Max told her, rubbing the panel of glass in the middle of the door and peering in.

'How do you know?'

He kicked the debris of dried leaves and twigs that had blown into the porch and lay piled up against the door. 'No self-respecting Yorkshire lady would have a front porch in this state,' Max told her wryly.

Was he joking? She didn't know but if he was to be believed and it was true they were in trouble if no one was home.

'Where are you going?' Justine wailed as suddenly he moved out of the protection of the covered porch to go round to the back of the cottage.

'To see if there's a window I can force open,' he called out, his voice barely audible over a whine of wind that suddenly screamed in her ear.

Justine stood there shivering and trembling with cold as flurries of wild snow encroached into the porch to lash at her face. Suddenly the reality of what he had just said hit her. She sped after him, nearly ricochetting into him round the side of the cottage. She steadied herself with one hand on the rough wall.

'Are you crazy or what?' she cried. 'You just can't force your way into other people's property.'

'I'm not forcing my way, not yet anyway. Be a sweetie and pop back to the car. There's a torch in the glove compartment——'

'We can't, Max,' she protested, almost dancing up and down with cold and fear that someone might come along and find them trying to get in.

Max was wrestling with a sash window and not having much success with his one arm.

'Don't, Max,' she pleaded, 'you'll hurt yourself.'

'It would help if I could see properly,' he grated. 'The torch, Justine.'

'You can't——'

Suddenly he grasped her shoulder and spoke fiercely, 'We must, Justine. We can't sit in the car all night. We'll run the battery flat by morning trying to keep warm. We're lost and we need shelter for the night and this cottage is it.'

A 'but' stayed frozen on her lips and then Justine didn't attempt to argue again. She was freezing and the snow wasn't flurrying any more. It was a blizzard and the wind was howling so much that her ears and jaw were already aching miserably. She could imagine what the biting cold was doing to Max's injured arm... He was right, they needed shelter for a while and surely the people that owned this cottage wouldn't want it any other way? She ran to the car and found the torch. Once she had it she remembered what he'd said about flat batteries and switched off the car lights.

'Justine, here.'

Justine swung the beam of the torch to where his voice came from. The front door was open and Max was standing grinning in the doorway.

Justine flew to him, straight into his arms. He held her comfortingly and to her astonishment she found she was shaking from head to toe and it wasn't with cold.

'Hey, what's wrong?' Max asked softly.

'Nerves, I think. I've . . . I've never broken into a house before.'

'And you haven't now,' he laughed. 'I did.'

She drew back from him, embarrassed that she'd thrown herself into his arms. 'But I'm an accomplice,' she whimpered.

'So, if we get caught we'll both go down for a long stretch.'

'This isn't a time to joke, Max,' she breathed nervously, swinging the torch beam around the tiny hallway. She saw a light switch and lunged for it. Nothing.

'Try this,' Max suggested, delving into his pocket and coming up with a handful of pound coins. 'I thought I saw a meter down there in the corner.'

Justine shone the torch around the floor and found the meter in the far corner.

'There, I told you this was a holiday cottage.'

Justine handed the torch to him and while he beamed it into the corner she squatted down and fed the meter and as the hall light blazed on she stood up and looked at him. His jeans were wet below his knees, his hair was dishevelled and dripping with melted snow and he was clutching his bad arm to his chest but at least he was smiling.

Justine couldn't look so self-satisfied.

'Max, what have we done?' she breathed worriedly.

'Got ourselves a night of board and lodging by the looks of it,' he said lightly.

'But we can't stay here the night,' she protested. 'Someone might already be staying here . . . they might just have popped out for the evening.'

Max grinned. 'Hardly, it's freezing in here, and, besides, look at that pile of junk mail on the doormat. No one's been here for ages.'

Justine shivered. She was nearly swayed by his reasoning but not completely. Max put the torch down on a chair and reached for her hand and squeezed it reassuringly.

'Let's have a look round and do something about warming the place up.'

Justine nodded because there was no choice but to go along with his suggestions, but she wasn't happy with it.

The cottage was tiny, just the one main room downstairs with a dog-leg staircase in it to the upper floor. Max was already on his way up. Behind the staircase was a latched door, slightly ajar, which led to a small kitchen-diner. The wind was howling in through the window which Max had left open. Justine slid it down and shivered again. She heard the creak of floorboards as Max moved around upstairs and it was the only good feeling about the place. She looked round the stone-floored kitchen.

It was well equipped and she found some teabags and coffee and some cans of food in the cupboard. She went through to the sitting-room to call up to Max that she had found some food but she said nothing because he was coming down the stairs, looking grim-faced, which Justine supposed was because the upstairs accommodation wasn't up to much.

'That bad, is it?' she tried to joke.

He gave her a hesitant smile. 'Very pretty, actually. Not to my taste but...' He shrugged and turned away from her. 'I think the first priority is to get a fire going.'

There was a wood-burning stove in the fireplace and stacked next to it was a pile of logs and some kindling and matches. Max went down on his knees on the hearth rug and opened the doors of the woodburner.

'Do you think we ought to?' Justine asked. 'I mean somebody might see the smoke from the chimney and come to investigate.'

'I doubt anyone can see a hand in front of their face in this blizzard,' he told her tightly. She wondered at the bitterness in his tone. A short while ago he had been smiling; now he was as poker-faced as that poker in the hearth. Suddenly he looked up at her. 'Justine, don't look so worried. No one would put a dog out on a night such as this. If somebody does come, which I doubt they will, we'll just tell them we're lost and took shelter.'

'But you broke in!'

His eyes narrowed and she saw the tensing of his jaw in sufferance. 'The window wasn't locked,' he snapped irritably. 'I didn't smash my way in but I would have done. We're lost on the moors, in a blizzard, and I don't intend perishing for the sake of your guilty conscience. Now do something helpful and see if there's an old newspaper around somewhere that I can start this fire with.

Justine frowned at his sudden flare of temper but without further protest she went back into the kitchen. There was a pile of old magazines on the work surface and a newspaper. She looked at the date, 23rd September. So no one had been here since then. She sighed in resignation. He was right, it was a holiday retreat and no one was holidaying here a few weeks before Christmas.

She took the paper in to him and knelt beside him to roll it up and knot it for him. Then she got to her feet.

'I'd better get the stuff in from the car.'

'I'm quite capable of doing that,' he bit out.

She could see he was struggling to set the fire with one hand and she knew she was not helping his manly pride by offering to get the bags from the car but it didn't stop her snapping back at him from the door.

'Don't be such a bloody martyr, Max. If it wasn't for your cussedness in insisting we took this route——'

'If you hadn't taken a wrong turning——'

'And if you hadn't smashed up your arm in some silly polo game we wouldn't be here now, breaking into other people's property!'

Oh, damn him! She hadn't meant to say that. He'd made her say it. His sudden short temper had fired her own fury. 'Oh, to hell with you!' she added suddenly, not regretting it one bit because he was looking at her as if she had just crawled out from the bark of that log he was holding in his hand.

She slammed out of the front door and slithered and fought her way to the car. It took her two journeys to bring all their bags in, by which time she was more concerned with her own wet, freezing discomfort than his hurt feelings. She needed the loo and God help him if it was an outside one!

'Did you find a bathroom upstairs on your travels?' she asked scathingly. He was still on his knees on the hearthrug. The fire in the burner blazed happily but the set of Max's shoulders as he studied the knobs on the side of the black stove showed he wasn't happy at all.

Without turning he muttered, 'See for yourself.'

Justine gave the back of his neck a withering look and then clomped up the stairs with her bag and let it drop to the floor on the tiny landing on the upper floor. Two latched doors. Her heart sank. A bathroom didn't exist. They probably didn't in these old cottages, so an outside loo was on the cards. At least she had a bed to sleep in, though. She opened the first door and groped for a switch. The room was perfect and Justine stepped into it with relief. It was decorated in pink and green chintz and had low white beams and the big double bed with its brass knobs looked so comfy and welcoming that she nearly flopped on it there and then.

'This will do for me,' she murmured to herself, going back to the landing for her bag. Female curiosity had her opening his bedroom door to see what it was like.

Justine stood rooted to the spot as she gaped into the . . . the bathroom. In pink and green to match the bedroom, it did nothing to cheer Justine. She closed her eyes in disbelief. There was only one bedroom and then slowly she opened her eyes as thoughts and realisations flooded her mind in confusion.

Max had been up here first. He knew there was only one bedroom, so why...? She stood by the pink handbasin and ran the tap. Ice-cold water juddered out and Justine wet her hands and rubbed them over her hot face. She wasn't freezing any more, she was running a fever with the realisation that had just rushed her. His attitude had changed after he had been up here. He had been snappy with her and surely if, as he had led her to believe, he wanted her, he wouldn't have been that way. He would have been...maybe triumphant at the thought that they would be forced to share that bed?

Well, he hadn't been triumphant, just grim-faced and as sour as an old crocodile with toothache. Bath and Chester crowded in on her. In Bath they had shared a suite but after the revelations about his secretary he had made no attempt to get her into his bed. And Chester, he had booked *two* rooms when one would have sufficed if he really had been keen to bed her. And now this, his po-faced attitude when finding the only bedroom in the cottage and his clear dread that he might have to share it with her.

Somewhere along the way he had decided he didn't want her after all. Somewhere along the way he had realised she wasn't the girl he had been attracted to and manipulated on this trip. So, shouldn't she be ecstatic about that? She should be, but the truth was she wasn't. The cold truth iced down her spine and she shivered again. Rejection for the third time? It loomed positively, and if he had regrets hers were a thousandfold more.

CHAPTER SIX

EVENTUALLY Justine went downstairs. Already the small sitting-room was warming up but she wasn't in the mood to appreciate it. Her eyes flicked around the room. The sort of furniture that graced it cried out 'holiday let'—a cottage suite upholstered in tapestry fabric with hard wooden arms, a sideboard, a teak coffee-table, all very basic and serviceable and comfortable enough. Her wide eyes lingered on the two-seater sofa. By no stretch of the imagination could she see herself or Max spending a restful night sprawled on that. But one of them would have to.

'I'll sleep down here,' she told him when she went through to the kitchen where he was filling the kettle. She took the kettle from him and plugged it in because it was difficult for him to do it with one hand.

He stepped back out of her way and leaned back against the work surface to watch her getting cups and teabags out of the cupboard.

'You're the driver so you'll need a good night's rest. I'll sleep down here,' he said decisively.

Well, if that wasn't confirmation that he had lost interest in her she didn't know what was. She couldn't help the tears spurting to her eyes but she could help them spilling. She swallowed hard.

'You can't sleep on that hard old thing with your bad arm——'

'Don't patronise me, Justine.' His voice was a warning growl.

Her anger was up at that and she slammed one of the cups unnecessarily hard down on the work surface. It shattered.

'I'm not patronising you, and now look what you've made me do!'

She gathered up the pieces and dashed them into a pedal bin by the door. 'And don't try to be so macho about that arm of yours,' she went on. 'So it hurts—admit it instead of biting at me every time I try to help you.' Again she was sorry for her outburst but she couldn't bring herself to apologise. He'd only think she was patronising him again. 'Take your painkillers and get out of here. This kitchen isn't big enough for the two of us.'

She reached up to the cupboard for another cup and he turned away from her and his voice was flat when he spoke.

'While you rustle up some supper I'll go up and take a shower.'

'Shower!'

'Yes, do you object to that?' he grated, eyeing her coldly from the door.

'Not at all, but isn't it a bit spartan showering in cold water—or are you just trying to prove how manly you are in spite of that arm?' She couldn't help niggling at him. Rejection did crazy things to you, like the last time when she had heaved that potted plant at his head. Now, in someone else's cottage, she had nothing to heave but insults.

'I don't have to prove my manhood to any woman, Justine,' he said slowly and determinedly, 'and you certainly don't urge me to take a cold shower; your biting sarcasm is a turn-off in itself. I'm going to take a *hot* shower. Didn't you notice there was an electric shower in the bathroom—or were you too busy up there coyly wondering how you were going to hang on to your modesty if we were forced to share that bed?'

'I... I was *not*!' she flamed.

'Just as well. I'll save you the trouble. It's all yours.'

Justine was left fuming. The kettle came to the boil, matching the steam that was coming out of her ears. She snapped it off and as the boiling water settled so did her fury. Once again she was engulfed by that crazy *frisson* of disappointment. Oh, hell, what was happening to her?

Realisation washed over her like a cold shower. She was falling in love with him, that was what was happening to her. Or had she already fallen, years ago at first sight of him? No, that had been just a teenage crush—hadn't it? But the pot-throwing incident...hadn't she been so frustrated that he hadn't been impressed with her a second time? Nothing to do with her talent but all to do with the male-female chemistry poets waxed lyrical over. She had felt it for him but he hadn't for her, and hell had no fury 'like a woman scorn'd'.

She was being scorned again and this time it was ten times worse than the others, because she knew him better now and the longing for him was growing deeper and he was a villain for leading her on at that dinner party and for manipulating her into agreeing to this trip.

But there were more immediate needs to be catered for, she thought sensibly. Food and drink and warmth. She checked the fire in the sitting-room and it was burning nicely. Max had closed the front doors of the wood burner and she guessed it would stay in through the night and keep her warm. She *would* sleep down here. No way could she expect him to.

She was stirring a concoction of baked beans and vegetable soup when he came down and into the kitchen.

'We take bread for granted, don't we?' she murmured without looking at him. 'What I'd give for a nice warm crusty baton to go with this.' She was making conversation but what else was there to do in this predicament?

He took the pan from her and slid it off the electric ring and she looked up at him in surprise. He looked refreshed, clean and relaxed and warm whereas she felt dishevelled and weary and half frozen from standing on the cold stone floor of the kitchen in wet loafers.

'Go up and have a shower,' he said quietly. 'I'll finish this off. You might even get a hot bath. The wood burner heats the water and the radiators upstairs. It's quite comfortable up there now.'

She didn't argue but murmured a 'thanks' as she turned away from him. The ache in her chest wasn't 'comfortable' as she plodded wearily up the stairs. She did love him, she supposed, because she couldn't feel such desolation if she didn't.

He was right, the radiators were warming up and there was hot water. She ran a bath and slowly undressed and when she lowered herself into the silky water she wondered how on earth she was going to cope with the rest of the trip.

Later when she came downstairs Max had set the teak coffee-table by the fire. Two bowls of steaming soup and a pot of tea and cups and saucers were waiting. A table lamp glowed on the sideboard and he'd opened the doors of the wood burner and the blazing logs were a welcome sight but Max didn't look very welcoming as he sat staring moodily into the flames while he waited for her.

He occupied the sofa so Justine took a cushion from one of the chairs and sat on it on the floor close to the table.

'Thanks for doing this,' she murmured picking up a soup spoon. 'It must have taken a dozen trips to bring this lot through with your bad arm.'

'For God's sake will you stop harping on about my bad arm?'

Eyes wide with surprise at his outburst, she stared at him for a brief second and then she let her spoon clatter down to the table.

'And what is it with you all of a sudden?' she blurted. 'You've used it to your advantage so far, so why the sudden change of heart?'

He looked at her solidly for a moment and then picked up his soup spoon. 'Perhaps that's just it, a sudden change of heart,' he grated morosely, and then started to eat.

Justine picked up her spoon but she couldn't even see her bowl through the mist of tears that suddenly welled. So that was it, what she had suspected, that he was now deeply regretting dragging her along on this trip.

'Justine.'

She looked up in surprise at the sudden softening of his tone.

'Why the tears?'

She bit her lip and quickly scooped up a spoonful of soup and swallowed it. 'It's this soup,' she gulped, hating him for noticing. 'It's too hot.'

'It has nothing to do with the soup. It's this place, isn't it?'

She looked around her and the tears were under control now. He'd never know the truth of it all. No, it wasn't this place. This tiny cosy cottage in the back of beyond with the snow falling outside was the most romantic place in the world for two lost lovers. Well, they were lost but they weren't lovers and never would be because he didn't want her.

'Well, it's a far cry from the hotel in Chester,' she retorted miserably. She bent her head over the soup again.

Max was close enough to lean down and scoop her hair back from her face. He held a strand of it between his finger and thumb and gently caressed its silky gloss and then let it go. She looked up at him, eyes wide with surprise at the sudden tenderness, and he was smiling.

'I'm sorry,' he offered softly, 'because it's all my fault. If I hadn't been so pigheaded about the route we'd be safely in Scotland by now.'

'I took a wrong turning and that's why we are here, as you so crassly reminded me a while back,' she hit back. She wasn't going to be placated by his soft apology. She was hurting too much inside to be placated.

'So whoever is at fault it doesn't matter because we're here and we have to make the best of it. It's not so bad, is it? We have some warmth and a roof over our heads and this soup is good, isn't it?' He picked up his spoon and started to eat again.

Justine shrugged, an admittance that it was. Yes, all was right with the world but all was wrong with how she was feeling inside, jumbled and hurt and wanting so much more than when they had started out on this trip.

They ate in silence and then Justine leaned back against one of the armchairs to drink her tea. She stared into the fire because to look at him would be torture.

'Tell me about your travels,' he said at last.

'Why?' she asked rather belligerently. He only wanted to hear to while away the time before bed.

'Because I'd like to hear what you've been up to since Belgravia.'

'I told you I've never been to Belgravia,' she retorted.

She was aware of him shrugging out of the corner of her eye as she stared grimly into the fire.

'It must have been someone else, then,' he said quietly. He reached out and touched her hair again, a small soothing gesture that so annoyed her that she jerked her head out of his reach.

'Don't do that!' Suddenly she was angry with him again. Why couldn't he just leave her alone now that he had decided he didn't want to know after all? Games again? The warmth and a full stomach mellowing him down to that teasing attitude of his again?

She struggled up from the floor, aching miserably now, bone-weary with the whole charade.

'What are you doing?'

'Clearing up! It's what I'm here for, isn't it? To be used and——'

'What the hell is wrong with you?' he suddenly blazed.

She glowered down at him and what had she got to lose by telling him the whole truth? Nothing but a bit of pride and she'd lost enough of that with him before, twice before!

'What the hell is wrong with *me*?' she stormed. 'Ask yourself the same question and you might get somewhere. You blow hot and cold like a clapped-out hairdrier. One minute you're joyfully breaking into someone else's house and then when you realise there's only one bedroom you're in the depths of a moody.' She took a deep breath. 'Max Benedict, I wouldn't sleep with you in that bed if you offered my father your damned contract for life——' Oh, strewth, what was she saying here? He didn't even want her in his bed!

Suddenly he was on his feet and his left arm swung her against him. His blazing anger was only inches from hers.

'I don't want you in that bed!'

Verbal confirmation stabbed through her, so viciously it took the breath from her lungs. She struggled for it, found it in the back of her throat.

'You've made that patently obvious!'

The power went out of him then and Justine felt the release and used it to her advantage. Without thinking she pushed him away from her, pushed at his strapped arm. Instantly she bit her lip in regret expecting to see a wince of pain shoot across his face, but he stood there only showing a second of shock in his eyes and then to her horror those eyes softened knowingly and she knew why. With that hissed-out statement she had left herself wide open. Now he knew what was bothering her, making her say things that were best left unsaid and he was going to enjoy putting her down again.

'And I don't care that you don't want me any more,' she blurted in defence. 'I know what you're thinking and you're wrong. I really don't care about that bed——' And now she was making it all worse. Her heated denial was an admittance in itself that she did care. She wasn't very clever with these sophisticated games. He was right, he could outwit her in every way....

'Justine...' Her name came out with compassion and he reached out and took her into his arm again. His lips were brushing her hair and she weakened and felt faint with this sudden turn of his moods again. 'Can't you see why I don't want you in that bed?' he whispered softly.

Was she supposed to answer that? Her head reeled with the cruelty of it.

'You don't have to tell me,' she cried, trying in vain to quell this feeling of weakness inside her. His hand in that paralysing spot in the small of her back was having its effect once again. Her legs were boneless, her heart was slowing dangerously. 'You don't like me...you don't want me...'

'It's the fact that I do want you that's spinning me out of control, Justine,' he whispered, grazing his warm mouth against her ears, her neck, her throat. His hand came up to the back of her neck and he held her head against his. 'I had every intention of seducing you when we set out——'

Her heart chilled. 'And...and now you can't bear the sight of me...'

He moved so he could look her in the face. His hand smoothed the side of her cheek and his eyes were smoky blue-grey with softness. 'No, not that, Justine, but something else that's worrying me senseless. I don't allow myself to get too emotionally involved with women, and I'm beginning to care for you far more than is good for the pair of us.'

Her heart started hammering wildly. He didn't know what he was saying...she didn't know what she was hearing! Slowly he lowered his mouth to hers and when their lips met she was more confused than ever. His kiss was slow and tender and seemed to be powered by feeling, real feeling. This she couldn't cope with, this about-turn of his affections after all that had happened since they had forced their way into this remote cottage.

She tore her mouth from his, but he tightened his hold on her in case she was about to escape.

'I don't understand,' she breathed hoarsely.

'I do want you, Justine, just as I said before. When I manipulated this trip I had every intention of making it with you along the way——'

The hurt was there again, the terrible fear of rejection again. It powered the weakness from her and gave her strength to bring her hand up to strike him for that.

Anger flared in his eyes and his reactions were as swift as a striking snake. He caught her wrist before it did any damage and wrenched her to him again. She felt the hardness of his body against her and was shocked at his arousal.

'I could take you now, Justine,' he grated. 'One arm or two, I could take you, and you'd let me because you want it as badly as I do...and don't you dare protest that you don't. It's what's powering your anger and fury now and it's what powered my anger and fury tonight. You're mad with me because you think I don't want you any more, aren't you?'

'I don't think, I *know*,' she whispered. 'You changed when you came downstairs. There...there's just the one bedroom...and...and you don't want to share it with me.'

'It's because I do that my mood changed, Justine. I want to make love to you in that bed but the need is different from before. Before you were a challenge——'

'And now you think the challenge is over and I'll come willingly and the sport is over for you.' Her eyes hardened. 'I'm just a game to you——'

'No, not a game, Justine, never that.' He took a deep breath. 'I've told you I don't get emotionally involved with my women and I find I'm getting emotionally involved with you. I'm beginning to care too damn much and that's a danger to us both.'

Her senses spun at that admission and her heart melted. The tension drained from her body. He cared for her, although it sounded as if he had conditions, but at the moment were those conditions to be considered? As his mouth came to hers again she didn't even want to think about them. All she knew was that she wanted him to hold her this way, to kiss her this way...to love her this way...however temporary it might be.

The kiss was long and impassioned and she slid her arms up around him and succumbed to the power of his sexuality. She let her body melt against him and her heart cry out her longing for him and when he shifted his mouth from hers and let out a small moan she couldn't bear the despair of it.

She brought her mouth back to his, to show him that she wanted him, but almost brutally he moved his lips away from her.

'No, Justine.' His voice was thick with emotion. 'Not like this. Not here. You deserve better.'

Her green eyes were shot with pain as she looked up at him. She shouldn't have done that, shown herself to be so willing. Embarrassment flooded the anger to her lips and the pain was gone from her eyes and anger shot them now. She stepped back, away from him so he could see the full force of her anger.

'It's just a game to you, isn't it? Life is a game to you, everything you do is a wretched game! You use people for your own amusement. You take advantage of that crook arm of yours——' His eyes narrowed warningly but Justine didn't care. 'You say I deserve better than this when the truth is you think you're too damned high and mighty to make love in a simple holiday cottage. It's luxury suites in luxury hotels for you——'

'Justine!'

She took another step back, then several more. 'Don't "Justine" me and don't you dare wind me up again, saying you care when it's just an excuse to get rid of me. So have it your own way, Max, but you can suffer for the mistake you made with me. You can suffer all night on that creaky old sofa because I don't care a toss for your useless arm or the rest of you come to that!'

And then she burst into tears and it couldn't have been worse if she had swooned at his feet. Shaking with anger at herself, she let out a stifled sob and fled from the room. She stumbled up the stairs, burst into the bedroom and threw herself down on the bed.

Suddenly the bedside lamp was snapped on and in the next instant she was being rolled over on to her back. Max stood over her, glowering down at her with that same look she had seen before...when she had heaved that pot of African violets at his head. That look had puzzled her then but now she recognised it. It wasn't shocked disbelief that someone had had the audacity to do such a thing but an arousal, a look of desire for someone with that sort of nerve. And now she was seeing it again. No one did or said those things to Max Benedict and it excited him.

'Max, no,' she pleaded, and tried to scrabble away from him. He caught her ankle and hauled her back to him. She lay motionless, not afraid any more, just curious to see what he would do next.

He did nothing but stare down at her as if wondering whether to chance his luck or not with a pot-throwing hysteric.

He spoke at last, with velvety smoothness. 'I'm not going to rape you, Justine, though I'm hungry enough for you.'

'Rape is an act of violence not a sexual act,' she blurted fiercely.

'Neither applicable in this case,' he murmured softly, and lifted her ankle slightly and lowered his head to her bare foot. His lips brushed across the arch of her foot and the sensation that it burned on her flesh ran the whole length of her sprawled body.

Instinctively she drew her foot back as if it had been stung. He smiled at her and then lowered himself to sit on the bed. Mesmerised, she watched him start to remove the strap from his injured arm and as he bent his head to shift it from around his neck she sat up, knowing why he was doing it. But understanding his motives was something else. Could she believe what he had said downstairs, that he did want her but things had changed, he was beginning to care too much? She wanted to, oh, so badly she wanted to believe that, and surely it was possible? Her mind flash-fired all the little things he had done and said since this trip had started. It seemed they had laughed a lot together, but they had argued a lot too, and wasn't that because of this sexual tension between them? Oh, yes, definitely that. And now he wanted her in spite of some obscure honour he had tried to show her. But didn't men say things like that, to show that they cared more than they actually did just to get women's compliance? So many questions and answers and did she have time to ponder them when her heart was beating so and her pulses were so heatedly raging with need?

'Let me do that,' she said softly, and it was just the thing he had been waiting for. As she moved towards him their eyes locked and there was all knowing in that soft exchange.

Justine didn't want to think any further than this moment as tenderly she removed the leather strap from around his neck and shoulders. As she leaned closer to him his mouth brushed her hair and then his arm was around her and his mouth was on hers once again. No barriers now, no confusing kisses, no doubts as to what they were doing. Both knew there was no going back, only further forward to what they both so desperately wanted.

Her lips parted to receive the full passion of his and her arms slid around his neck to hold him firmly against her. Her need for him rose swiftly and passionately as she had always expected it would. In her fantasies it had always been this way, fiery and urgent, but her fantasies had never taken into account this rush of love and tenderness as well. It was a confusing feeling, the urgency countered with this new softness inside her. She wanted to love him as well as satisfy this deep hunger. She wanted it to last forever and yet she wanted him to take her in the heat of his passion, swiftly, thoroughly, impatiently.

His hand moved from her back to the front of her sweater. It ran lightly over her breast and as she swelled with need his touch deepened till his caress was almost a pain. He eased her back against the pillows and his mouth was urgent this time, tearing hungrily at her lips. He eased her sweater up to her shoulders and lowered his head to draw passionately on her engorged nipples till she arched helplessly against him, writhing and letting out small heated moans of intense pleasure.

And then she felt the tension run through his body. It rippled down him, from his shoulders and beyond, and she knew it wasn't the tension before the rejection. His injured arm was a barrier between their heated bodies. It lay heavy and useless against her and she knew the tension was an anger within him, for himself, and she knew if it came to the surface it would undermine him and his pride would force him away from her love. But to take over would undermine him further and she didn't know how to ease the misery for him.

Her hands came up and gently she lifted his head from her breasts and covered his mouth with hers. She ran her hands down the side of his face, down his throat till she reached his shirt-front. Still holding her lips to his, she unbuttoned his shirt and then his hand came across to still her. He drew back from her then and her heart seized, fearing this rejection and yet knowing what was causing it. She wanted to tell him that it was all right, that she understood and she would help him, but no words came to her lips, they just parted, glistening with dewy moisture as she stared in wonderment at him.

He stood by the bed and slowly started to undress himself, watching her face as every action was executed with smoothness and dexterity. He shed his shirt and let it slide to the floor and Justine resisted the urge to lean forward and press her lips to his magnificent chest. Instead she kneeled up on the bed and slowly and languorously she lifted her sweater over her head. His hand stilled on the buckle of his belt as she revealed her naked breasts. He gave a sharp intake of breath and leaned towards her to pull her closer to him so that he could kiss each breast in turn, to suckle each nipple gently till her desire was white-hot inside her.

He drew back from her again and slowly but surely undid his belt. Justine smiled and knew how much he was enjoying this tease. She burned inside, relished the ache of need deep in her groin. As he unzipped his jeans she watched him unwaveringly and then slid her hands down her hips and eased her leggings down over her thighs. Again he reached for her and, sliding his hand around her waist, pulled her forcibly from the bed till she was standing next to him. She kicked out of her leggings as his lips parted hers, hungry with desire to taste her, to draw on the inner sweetness of her lower lip. Justine clung to him, loving the desire that strained their bodies hard against each other.

He slid his hand into the back of her lace briefs and urged her ever harder against him till she wanted to drown with the pleasure his arousal shuddered through her. She hardly felt the removal of her briefs as he combined it with moving rhythmically against her, driving her senses wild with the promise of what was to come. She felt a flood of fiery energy as her naked skin burned against the silk of what remained between them.

'Allow me this,' she murmured throatily as with trembling fingers she eased his silk boxer shorts from his narrow hips.

He gave a small soft laugh of submission and then she heard a deep shuddering gasp as she took him completely unawares by running her hands down over his hips and then to his arousal, taking it in her hands and caressing it tenderly. He moved against her, holding her by the small of the back, grazing hot kisses across her face till they were both trembling with need.

Gently Max tumbled her back on the bed and, still standing but supporting his weight with his hand on the bed, he leaned over her and started to kiss her body. Slowly and sensuously he ran his tongue over the column of her throat, kissed the scented hollow at the base of her throat then trailed his warm lips down over her breasts. Justine closed her eyes in sheer ecstasy as he mouthed kisses across the flat planes of her stomach, buried his face in the silky dark hair between her thighs till she was gasping and twisting with desire. Then he eased up and was touching her, stroking her between her thighs as she lay straddled on the edge of the bed, driving her further and further till she could hold back no longer. She wanted release, she wanted him inside her, she wanted him to love her...

She opened her eyes as she felt the loss of the warmth of his kisses, of the withdrawal of his caresses from her inner thighs, she opened her eyes in time to see him looking down on her, his eyes hooded with such deep desire that love and hope filled her heart with joy. He bent over her again, supporting himself with his good arm and, still standing, he slid into her silky warmth as smoothly and as easily as if they had been made for each other. The power and urgency of his thrusts urged her up from the bed to fling her arms around his neck, to hold him, to move with him, to give him every deep part of her in a union that was feverish and urgent, a tumultuous consummation of heated pleasure that fired their blood till only the inevitable could save them from a boiling inferno. It came with the power of a volcano, an eruption that shook the breath from their bodies, an earth-shattering climax of white-hot liquid fire that burst inside them as their lips met in a simultaneous gesture of complete oneness.

He collapsed beside her on the bed and drew her into his side and cradled her against him with his left arm. Justine nestled her mouth into his neck and grazed it with soft kisses, soothing the fiery pulse in his throat till it settled into a soft rhythm. She felt the pressure ease from his strained body and only then did she realise the physical effort that their lovemaking had cost him.

Nervously she ran her hand across his chest. His skin burned as if in a fever and though his breath was even now it hadn't been minutes ago. She sensed that he was already asleep so gingerly she reached for a blanket that was folded at the end of the bed and pulled it up over them. She slid her hand under the blanket and lay her arm across his chest again. It was then her fingers came into contact with his injured arm which lay limp across his waist. Tenderly she ran her fingers down the arm, feeling the warmth above his elbow, the heat of the deep scar and then... Justine's own blood ran cold. His arm from the elbow down felt different, cooler, but what had brought a chill to her own heart was his hand and his numb fingers. They were as icy cold as the snow that had driven them here. In sharp contrast to the heat of the rest of his body they were cold and lifeless. It was from that moment on that Justine began to wonder, and it thrust sleep from her for the rest of the night. Reasons for his change of moods, for his admittance to the blues when he had phoned her to arrange this trip all jumbled and made her ache with worry. Was his next operation a last-hope attempt to get back the use of his arm? And if it failed? Oh, dear God, Max Benedict wouldn't be able to cope with that... not without help.

CHAPTER SEVEN

JUSTINE awoke to a blinding brightness and she remembered the blizzard of the night before. The snow outside was reflected off the white-beamed ceiling and the white walls and Justine blinked her eyes getting used to the light.

She was alone in the brass-knobbed bed and her first concern was for Max. She hoped he wasn't doing something silly like trying to dig the car out of a snowdrift single-handed. Single-handed. Those two words jarred through her painfully, reminding her of why she'd had such a troubled night, only dropping off in the early hours of the morning, exhausted with worry about Max's lifeless hand.

Leaping out of bed, she snatched at her robe and, pulling it round her, went to the window. She was amazed to see only a couple of inches of snow instead of the expected drifts and further amazed to see a Land Rover parked behind the Jaguar with a couple of border collies yapping in the back of it.

She went to the landing and stopped at the sound of voices. There was laughter and Max calling out a 'thanks' and then the thud of the front door being shut. She ran downstairs.

The sitting-room was warm, logs burned brightly behind the glass doors of the wood burner and she felt guilty for sleeping when she should have been down here stoking the fire. She went through to the kitchen and last night's washing-up had been done and Max was at the cooker grilling bacon...grilling bacon?

'Who was that?'

Max turned and smiled at her. 'The archangel Gabriel himself.'

'Seriously,' she snapped impatiently.

'My, you're sweetness and light first thing in the morning.'

'Sorry,' she mumbled, pushing her unruly hair from her face. 'You make me feel guilty for sleeping when I should have been down here clearing up and seeing to the fire. Who was that in the Land Rover?'

'Gabriel Harris, the farmer next door. If we'd gone another half-mile up the track we would have come to the farmhouse. He saw the smoke from the chimney and came straight down thinking the owners were here. He brought supplies.' He nodded to the worktop. 'Fresh milk, butter, eggs, bacon, black pudding and a crusty loaf straight out of the oven.'

Justine stood by him as with his left hand he deftly cracked an egg on the side of the pan and plopped it into hot butter next to the gently sizzling black pudding.

'Did he mind us being here?' she asked worriedly, not yet able fully to appreciate that Max was cooking a *real* breakfast.

'He understood when I explained and offered to leave a cheque for the owners. He wouldn't let me pay for the food, though.'

'That was kind of him and... and it was kind of you to see to the fire and... and clear up after last night.' Her eyes went to his bad arm and she relived the moment when she had touched his cold hand last night as he'd slept and her face went pale.

'What's wrong?'

'Nothing,' she shrugged. 'Move over and let me do this.'

She felt him stiffen and knew she had said the wrong thing. His pride again.

'Cut the bread,' he said brittly, 'that's something I can't do with one hand.'

'But there's plenty you can do very successfully with one,' she teased meaningfully. It was her first reference to their lovemaking last night and she hoped he would take it in the vein it was said, light-heartedly.

He gave her a sidelong glance as if he wasn't sure how to take it and then his lips slid into a very thin smile and she knew she had done wrong again. Making love wasn't something to be dismissed so lightly, it wasn't something to be dismissed—period.

'Do you want to talk about it?' she murmured as she set about slicing the still warm bread.

He laughed ruefully. 'Like "did the earth move for you?"'

Justine's hand froze around the bread knife. She would never have put those words into his mouth, not ever. Had he actually said them or was this whole trip sending her quietly mad?

'Well, you certainly have a nice line in "morning after the night before" chat. Remind me to jot it down in my little red book as a truly original piece of dialogue,' she said with scathing sarcasm. With a renewed feverishness she set about the loaf as if she was slicing through his neck.

'So what did you expect——?'

'I expected less of your bloody boring self-pity, Max Benedict,' she interrupted.

'And who's talking of self-pity, for pity's sake?' He brandished the fish slice in her direction. 'You, Justine,' he accused, 'you are the one hammering away at my supposed self-pity and feeling guilty for my getting up before you to stoke the fire and clear up and now you're trying to take over the cooking of this breakfast. I don't need wet-nursing, thank you!'

Justine brandished the bread knife at him in exchange, her eyes bright with anger. 'Oh, no? You needed a driver badly enough though, and you needed me to cut up your food for you that night of the dinner party badly enough. You were piling on the "poor wounded soldier" scenario then, weren't you? And I fell for it——'

'Yes, you fell, and aren't you just lapping it all up, putting me in my place for my dismissal of you months back? So, the earth didn't move for you last night—so why did you do it, Justine, because you felt sorry for me?'

Stunned, Justine stared at him in disbelief. Never would she have expected this from him. Not the Max Benedict she had built her dreams on, not the mega-Max who was so powerful, so successful. Slowly the truth dawned on her and she saw the terrible fear that he was hiding from the world, the fear that he might never get the use of his hand back. This was what was making him so wretchedly unbearable this morning and she wanted to rush at him and hold him and make it all right for him. Instead she swallowed hard and said what came naturally to her when he made her so damned mad she could kill for it.

'No, actually, I didn't feel sorry for you,' she said smoothly. 'I was just madly curious to know how a man with one arm made it! Satisfied?'

She didn't give him space to answer that; the narrowing of his blue eyes was enough to have her tossing the sliced bread into the frying-pan where the egg had fried itself to glutinous mass. She added cheekily, 'Good in bed you might be, good in the kitchen you ain't!'

She flounced off and had reached the bedroom and was furiously stripping the blanket from the bed when suddenly she was toppled from behind. She fell on to the bed. Max twisted her round to face him, pinning her under him with a force that took the breath from her.

'You make me so mad I want to make love to you forever!' he growled.

She pummelled hard on his good shoulder. 'And you make me so mad I could break your other arm!' she hissed through clenched teeth.

'It took a horse to snap this one,' he said heatedly, shrugging his bad shoulder. 'You couldn't match that if you ate hay packed with steroids by the bucketful.'

'I'd rather eat hay *and* steroids *and* the bucket than one of your beastly breakfasts!'

His mouth covered hers in a kiss that sapped the last of her temper from her. She felt the last of his temper draining from him too and what was left was the passion of the night before. The urgency and the need to repeat again and again all the delights they had savoured—and some more.

Justine clung to him, raked her fingers through his hair and let her love and desire wash through her unhindered by thoughts that this couldn't possibly last. No, she wouldn't think that way, that she was just another of his women to be used. She couldn't think that way because it wasn't that way, it couldn't be. Not with this feeling between them. It was too strong and too overpowering and too beautiful.

So dazed was she by the assault on her senses that she hardly noticed that during that impassioned kiss he had shifted his position to lie next to her not on top of her. He slid his hand under her robe and smoothed his hand so sensuously across her burning flesh that she thought she would die with the sweet pleasure it laced through her. Clinging to him, she mouthed kisses across his face and throat, drawing small moans of pleasure from him.

She felt his hand shift to the buckle of his belt and instinctively her hands went to help him. He let her and she felt a small victory beating like wings in her heart and it gave her courage.

'Let me,' she whispered softly.

'My pleasure,' he whispered back, so tenderly it allayed any doubts.

Justine took the initiative and she had never experienced anything quite so sensual in her life. Slowly she undressed him, smoothing kisses over his chest as she drew his shirt aside. She loved the smell of him, the firmness of his muscled flesh against her mouth, her face, her breasts. She adored every part of him, teased him with gentle nips, ran the tip of her tongue over his stomach till he laughed softly and squirmed under her. Delicately she ran her lips over his bad arm as it lay across his waist. Softly she kissed the scar at his elbow, kissed his wrist, and then she took his numb hand in hers and tenderly kissed each finger in turn, silently willing strength to the fingers that were lifeless. She felt a warmth in them that hadn't been there the night before and her heart swelled with hope and she felt a new happiness glowing inside, a happiness and a hope for him, and she knew that whatever happened, whatever the outcome, she would always love him and she would always be there for him if he wanted her to be and it had nothing, no, nothing to do with that awful word pity. She knew because it was something he didn't know, that she had loved him before, from the first moment she had set eyes on him.

Her body beneath her open robe glistened with desire and his breath was coming quicker and she needed him so badly but suddenly she was unsure of what to do. She had never loved a man this way, taking the lead, the giver not the taker. It was a delicious feeling with a tingling sense of power adding excitement and a new dimension to the intimacy of making love but she didn't want it to go wrong and it could so easily do so if she moved clumsily. She wanted it to be right, to be beautiful and sensuous, to flow like a choreographed ballet but...she didn't know the movements...was unsure of the positions...

Max sensed her uncertainty and with an encouraging smile and a soft unobtrusive gesture he moved her across him till she was straddling him. Her robe fell around them, cocooning them both in a satiny, warm-scented vacuum. She lowered herself over him and he guided himself into her silky moistness and the perfect union brought a gasp of sheer ecstasy from both their lips. Justine let her head drop forward with the intensity of feeling that spiralled through her. She couldn't look at him because he would know that she adored him, that the intensity of their lovemaking was something so very, very special in her life. He was her life, the pivot of her very being.

He touched her chin and lifted her head and murmured softly, 'Don't be shy. Look at me, Justine. I want to see your face as we make love.'

She opened her eyes and couldn't have disguised her adoration if she had tried. He moved his hips against her, small encouraging movements, watching her all the time, his blue eyes intense, his eyelids heavy with desire.

Biting her lower lip, she acknowledged his encouragement and moved with him, slowly at first, small rubbing movements that were so deeply intense with feeling that her breath caught in her throat till she could hardly breathe at all. And then the heat and the fire of a much deeper need raged through her, driving her on until their insatiable wanting was all, thrusting them deeper and harder into a state of blinding passion where nothing mattered but the giving of each other to each other. The power of their climax was so heady, so unreal, so deeply devastating that Justine cried out as if in pain and Max reached up for her and crushed his mouth to hers, to savour the intensity, to prolong the ecstasy, to soothe that last shuddering cry on her lips.

Justine collapsed beside him, breathing deeply to try and steady the rush of deep emotion that racked through her trembling body, and Max turned and with a moan of pleasure and deep satisfaction he gathered her fiercely against him and they lay that way for a long time.

Later he murmured against her cheek. 'You know we'll have to cut out this fighting or we'll never get to Scotland.'

She smiled and lifted her head to look down on him. She didn't want to be reminded of their mission, she wanted to stay here in this cottage forever, just like this, with Max holding her so possessively against him, as if they belonged together and he never wanted to let her go.

'I'm glad we took the scenic route,' she murmured.

'It would have been a lot safer if we'd kept to the motorways,' he admitted.

Was that spoken with regret? Justine wondered. She didn't want to contemplate the whys or wherefores. She didn't want to analyse and look for reasons, she didn't want to think beyond this moment, this cocoon of time and being, where an outside world existed beyond the stone walls of this cottage. There would be plenty of time for that later. For now she had no regrets. She couldn't regret something that was so sublimely beautiful, so incredibly intoxicating that she never wanted to sober.

'You shower and I'll get on with the breakfast which you so rudely interrupted,' he teased. He kissed the top of her nose. 'Out, woman, before I'm tempted to ravish you again.'

'I ravished you,' she laughed as she slid off the bed. 'And I hope you turned off the cooker before you came storming up here like a wild thing. This trip could cost you a fortune in compensation for damage done.'

'I've already paid,' she thought she heard him murmur, and then decided she had misheard because it didn't make sense.

And who would compensate the damage to her heart? she wondered later as she showered. Though that was a negative thought. She was already contemplating defeat before she had given him a chance. But what was she expecting? Max's love, Max's devotion, Max's paper contract... She shuddered deeply as she shampooed her hair. Forget the contract; it had no place in their lives. It was the reason they had undertaken this trip together in the first place but it was all different now, very different.

Justine gazed out over the misty loch. They'd had a fall of snow here on the west coast of Scotland as well but not enough to seize up the roads. The pine forests that towered over the perimeters of the loch shimmered through the grey mist, black with a dusting of white, ethereal and breathtakingly beautiful. But everything was beautiful to Justine's eyes. Even sight of the ugly Hammond Mill buildings in the distance on the edge of the water had a certain charm she hadn't noticed before.

From the huge plate-glass picture window of the Scandinavian-style lodge her father had built for the family Justine could see a convoy of trucks bringing the imported wood from Finland in from the port. She hugged herself and smiled. Max was over there at the mill and would be watching the delivery and then the mill manager, Greg Kendon, would show him around the works and then they would spend an age talking because Greg knew what he was up against in selling Hammond Paper. Not that he had a product on his hands that needed the hard-sell approach. No one could doubt the quality of their paper—it was second to none—but most buyers these days were more concerned with costing than quality.

She sighed and turned away from the window. But Max had no problems with costings. He could afford their product—it was just a question of did he want to? She wondered how far their affair would affect his decision and hated herself instantly for even considering it. Nothing had changed really. Max would do as he thought fit and their affair had nothing to do with it.

She made herself a coffee and settled down in the pine-floored sitting-room to wait for Max to return. She flicked through a magazine to pass the time but it hung heavily and she cast the magazine aside and sprawled flat out on the tan leather sofa and let her heart and her thoughts drift to Max.

There had been no more fighting since the cottage on the moors, just a lot of laughter and a lot of long pensive silences that hadn't been at all threatening because you couldn't be animated all the time. Their last overnight stop in Oban had been as magical as the cottage though very different. The hotel had been sumptuous, the food and wine in the restaurant a fitting prelude to the night's lovemaking.

And *lovemaking* it had been. Not sex, no, not that. You couldn't call what they had done and experienced the thrill of 'just sex'. No, it was love, though no verbal confirmation had taken place because there had been no need. Justine just knew he felt the same way as she did, that something beautiful had happened for them both.

She awoke to small tender kisses on her brow and she blinked open her eyes and it was dark but for a small lamp glowing on the sofa table and the flickering flames from the log fire.

Justine struggled out of a deep sleep and smiled up at Max looking so . . . no, not tenderly down on her . . . wearily. She sat up quickly and hurled her unruly hair back from her face, her guilt for having fallen asleep while he was spending a miserable, cold, exhausting time touring the works powering her to her feet.

'You're exhausted and I haven't even got the dinner on. Strewth, I'll have to microwave it now, can you bear that? It's a casserole and I hate microwaved food but you must be cold and hungry and your arm must be aching and I'd make a terrible . . .' Her voice dried in her throat as she stared at him, still muffled by a thick woolly scarf she had insisted he wore over his sheepskin before going to the mill. Dear God, but she had nearly said wife . . . that she would make a terrible wife!

She laughed quickly and added, 'Housekeeper!' hoping he hadn't noticed the rift in the exclamation.

He slumped down on to the sofa, so wearily that she supposed he hadn't.

'God, but that place is like a fridge,' he sighed.

Justine grinned and unwound the scarf from his throat and bent to kiss him warmly on the lips. 'The whole of Scotland at this time of the year is like a fridge,' she joked, and he smiled thinly. 'Did Greg drop you back? Let me pour you a drink to warm you. Brandy or Scotch?'

She didn't wait for an answer but her hands stilled on the bottle of brandy on the sideboard the other side of the room. There wasn't an answer coming and she realised he had said very little since wakening her. He seemed miles away, not with her at all, probably preoccupied with the mill, or... or was it something else? She didn't know, couldn't imagine what could be troubling him.

She handed him his brandy and he smiled up at her but it wasn't a smile that warmed her and filled her with a good feeling. It was a conciliatory sort of smile that puzzled her.

'Sit there and warm yourself—I'll get on with the dinner.' Taking her brandy, she went downstairs to the kitchen on the ground floor. The lodge had been built with the living area on the upper floor to take full advantage of the spectacular views and she pondered on the good sense of that as she worked because to ponder on Max's sombre mood would trouble her.

'We have to get back first thing in the morning,' Max said from the doorway.

Justine swung round from the microwave and gazed at him in surprise. He'd discarded his jacket and was leaning on the door-jamb, leaning with his bad shoulder against the pine surround and holding his glass of brandy in the left. There was something troubling him and all manner of reasons flooded her mind, the foremost was that he had seen nothing good at the mill to cause him any joy. She felt the loss for her father and even a grinding sympathy for Richard's dashed hopes. She gave no thought to herself for somehow she was small consideration at the moment.

'OK, if that's what you want I'll pack up the car tonight.' Justine turned back to the microwave to punch out the timer, her heart beating dully at the thought that he couldn't get away fast enough. They had planned on staying at the lodge for a couple of days, Max saying that he needed a couple of days at least in talks with Greg, but that was before the initial visit. Now the initial visit was over and he wanted to leave and that meant...

'Forget the car, we're flying back.'

She spun to face him, stunned by that. 'But you don't fly!' she blurted. 'You said...you said you had a pathological fear of it!'

He shrugged. 'I lied.'

'You lied?' Justine exploded, stepping towards him, her eyes widened with shock. 'You don't lie about things like that—and why? Why lie? There was no reason to.'

He heaved himself away from the door and put his brandy glass down on the worktop before meeting her in the middle of the vast kitchen. His arm gathered her around the waist and she wanted to pull away but didn't because his eyes were suddenly soft and persuasive.

'There was every reason to,' he told her warmly. 'If I hadn't your fearful brother-in-law would have accompanied me up here and that wasn't what I wanted.'

She stiffened against him, not understanding, and when he squeezed her as if to squeeze some thoughtful reasoning into her she realised what he was getting at.

'You lied to get me to drive you up here?' she cried incredulously. 'You lied about your fear of flying and not being happy with rail travel *and* you lied about not liking motorway travel!'

'No, not the dreaded motorways. That was the truth,' he laughed.

'All to get me to drive you up here.' She linked her arms around his neck and pressed her warm face against his. 'You are quite ruthless,' she murmured. 'Quite the most ruthless, conniving one-armed bandit it has been my misfortune to——'

'Seduce,' he finished for her, strengthening his hold on her, brushing his mouth lovingly against her hair and pressing his body intimately into hers, leaving her in no doubt that he wanted her and wasn't prepared to wait.

At last she eased out of his loving embrace and as she reset the timer of the microwave, giving the casserole longer than it required, she felt immeasurably flattered that he had wanted her enough to lie through his back teeth to get her. One tiny thought hovered on the periphery of her pleasure, and it was only a tiny thought, easily dismissed. If he had lied about that he was capable of unscrupulously lying about other things, other things being what he felt for her. But that thought was indeed easily dismissed because he had never actually voiced how deeply he did care for her anyway so therefore no lie had been spoken. She was happy with that for the time being because if he had proclaimed undying love she would be doubting his sincerity on this latest admittance.

As he kissed her tenderly when they stood by the bed she thought fleetingly that when you were so deeply in love you could find excuses for everything and the reason Max hadn't said he loved her was because he didn't have to. His kisses and his obvious need for her as hungrily he drew his mouth across hers was answer enough. He loved her. She was sure.

Justine hated leaving the lodge so hurriedly the next morning. It had never bothered her before, in fact she had always been glad to see the back of the Scottish mists and the rain when they had holidayed up here, but this time was different. She was with Max and because of her love for him the whole world was a glorious place to be. She wanted to stay, with him, just a few more days, because she somehow felt cheated. She had looked forward to the drive back. She had anticipated just as many precious moments as they had experienced on the way up and more. She loved him and wanted to be with him, though he was a bit of a grouch this morning, but she would suffer him because of her love.

'We haven't time for that, Justine,' he snapped impatiently as she hurriedly tidied up before the taxi came for them. 'Surely your father employs someone to look after this place when he's not here?'

'Yes, he does, but there's no reason to leave the place like a tip and you've got a lot in common with my sister, you know. She's always reminding me of my supposed status. I'm sure you'd get on extremely well with her.'

He glared at her and Justine wished she hadn't said that because it sounded as if getting to know her sister better was a consideration for the future. It hit her then, so painfully it was like a blow to her stomach, the thought that she was thinking on the lines of this being an ongoing relationship. But it was, surely?

Doubts...they suddenly materialised like wicked gremlins. She pummelled the cushions on the sofa and spread them around and reminded herself that she knew what she had let herself in for on this trip and she shouldn't be thinking so positively about a future with him. But the trouble was she was thinking of a deeper commitment because he had led her to believe that this was something special between them. Hadn't he said in that tiny cottage that he was beginning to care too much for her and it was dangerous for them both? The fact that they had let go and let their hearts rule their heads surely meant...

Suddenly she looked up at him, grasping a cushion to her chest for some security and comfort.

'You didn't get around to telling me why we suddenly have to leave,' she whispered hoarsely. Was it because he had suddenly realised they were getting in too deep? She held her breath, unable to coordinate her brain with her heart.

He bent to rummage in his holdall that she had packed so carefully for him a short while ago, so avoiding her gaze. 'Well, last night we were rather otherwise occupied,' he said in a low voice.

Justine felt a small, sharp pain in her heart. That had been spoken slightly derisively, as if all there was to this was sex. But no, she was on the defensive and looking for trouble and he hadn't meant it that way at all—he couldn't have.

'It wasn't a sudden decision,' he went on. 'I had it in mind from the off. As you know I've been keeping in touch with my secretary and——'

'"Sweetheart", you mean?'

'That's enough, Justine.'

Justine's blood ran cold. He sounded like Richard.

'There are a few problems that I knew were coming up,' he went on, 'and I need to get them sorted before the operation——'

'The operation!' she echoed, her voice seeming to bounce off the wooden panelling and coming back to hit her between the eyes. Was that the reason for this change in him, this abrupt, matter-of-fact, throwaway attitude he was taking with her? Was he trying to sound oh, so brave when he must be dreading the outcome, terrified it wouldn't be successful? It must be that, she reasoned, and her heart went out to him.

He zipped up the bag after not finding what he wanted and obviously thinking she was incapable of anything apart from making childish retorts and warming his bed to the right temperature. Justine dropped the cushion and rubbed at her brow feverishly. She had flipped. He couldn't be thinking anything of the sort. She was just raw with hurt and the thought of rejection and it was a possibility after all. Oh, God, anything was possible with this man. Rejection crying out above all else.

She moved to him. 'You didn't tell me the operation was imminent,' she whispered. 'When is it?'

'Next week, and I've got a helluva a lot to get through before I go in,' he told her brusquely.

Yes, because you might not be able to cope if it all goes badly, Justine thought in a panic. She understood what he must be going through, the fear and the uncertainty, but was there any need to treat her so coldly? Didn't he know that it would make no difference to her and really it should make no difference to him if she was beside him to love and support him? But that was asking too much of any man, and especially Max Benedict. Since when had the true love of a woman meant anything to him? Look how dismissively he had dealt with Beverley when her use and her smothering mothering had got too much for him.

'It'll be all right, you know,' she found herself saying and she reached out tenderly to run her fingers over the strap that held his arm to his chest and knew when he stiffened that she had made a very wrong move.

'I've absolutely no doubt that it will be,' he said dismissively. 'Now, sweetheart, will you get a move on? Oh, and where are the keys to the Jag? Greg is driving the car down for me during the week.'

Justine moved like an automaton from then on. 'Sweetheart'—he hadn't called her that since whenever and he hadn't said it since she had questioned the dubious nature of his relationship with his secretary. A term of endearment, he had explained, reserved for someone he was fond of. Trouble was, *fond* wasn't enough for Justine, no, not nearly enough, but it looked as if it was all she was going to get, and the thought numbed her through and through.

She didn't question the Jaguar-and-Greg arrangement; she said nothing, felt nothing, not even the pain of rejection, because when you had been dealt a body blow like that it felt remarkably like a debilitating general anaesthetic, blocking out life and reason and leaving you floating aimlessly in a surreal state of stupor.

CHAPTER EIGHT

BY THE time they were settled on their flight Justine was in the recovery-room of her senses.

Her body was throbbing with awareness now and a jumble of thoughts were gradually unravelling and it was becoming clear that she had been a blind, childish, naïve idiot to believe that anything good would come out of this relationship.

'You never did get round to telling me about your travelling days,' Max said beside her as the air hostess came round with drinks.

Justine shrugged. She was coherent now, fully. Absolutely composed, and she would show him that she cared as little as he did.

'It was fun. Four of us worked our way through Europe. Grape-picking, working in bars, hitch-hiking, working in bars.'

He laughed softly. 'Sounds fascinating.'

She doubted the sincerity of that statement but it didn't stop her going on. 'It was. I got to meet real people, kind, unpretentious people, people who lived simply and were happy with that.' She wondered if he was getting the point and then wondered what point she was trying to make and confusion hurried her on. 'We managed to get a job on a ship out of Portugal that was going to South America; by then we were two. We met a Spaniard on board who offered us work in Colombia.'

'Drug-running?'

She knew he wasn't serious. 'People always connect Colombia with drugs,' she said. 'They farm other things as well as dope, you know.'

'Grape-picking again?'

She smiled because he was attempting to be cheerful and while she could still summon a smile she might be all right. 'No. Santes ran an orphanage and I taught English there for a while. I'd picked up Spanish on our travels and a bit of Portuguese.'

'And what about your photography?'

Was he really interested or just making conversation? She sipped the drink Max had ordered for her. This was like a conversation between two strangers on a flight, not two people who had been lovers this past week. The hurt was beginning to seep back and she didn't want him to know that she couldn't cope if when they got off this flight he simply said 'see you some time'.

'I never stopped taking pictures all through my travels. I was already planning my photo library for when I returned.'

Suddenly his hand reached out for hers and he held it on the armrest between them. 'I'm sorry about that——'

'Yes, you've already said,' she interjected quickly.

'Your work is good, you know, and——'

'But not good enough——'

'I didn't say that——'

'Don't let's argue about it,' she said firmly and finally, and pulled her hand out from under his.

She felt the tension in him; she couldn't fail to notice it, knowing him so intimately now. He drained his drink and she drained hers and it seemed to be symbolic somehow. The end of everything.

'So what do you plan to do with the rest of your life?' he asked.

Oh, God, it *was* the end of everything. That was hardly the question you would ask the woman you wanted to share the rest of your life with, the woman you loved and wanted to be with. He didn't care for her, not one bit. It had all been a game. She had been someone to have fun with, and they had had fun; whatever they were thinking and regretting now, a lot of it had been fun.

'I want to start again,' she told him and that was an ironic thing to say under the circumstances of his third rejection of her. 'I made the mistake of taking on other people's talent and couldn't sustain them with the small amount of work I was getting in.' She paused before going on, picking her words carefully, speaking them slowly and deliberately. 'This time I'm going solo. I don't want or need anyone else in my life or my work.'

She turned slightly and looked at him but he wasn't looking at her. His head was against the headrest and his eyes were closed but she knew he was awake. She had wanted to hurt him with her double-edged conviction but he couldn't be hurt because he didn't care. Biting her lip, she closed her eyes too. She didn't care either she tried to convince herself before they touched down at Heathrow but as the undercarriage finally juddered down on the tarmac the bottom fell out of her world.

'But he must have said something!' Teresa urged at dinner that night. They were dining alone.

Richard and her father had decided to stay on in Brussels for another couple of days and Teresa, bored by then, had flown home alone.

Justine hadn't expected to find anyone home but Janet when she got back from Max's house where she had stopped off to pick up Teresa's Volvo, so her sister's presence was an unwanted shock on top of everything else.

Max had had the audacity to take her in his arms as she was leaving. Said she looked pale and tired and had tried to take the blame on himself.

'I've expected too much of you, Justine,' he said softly.

Brightly she retorted she was perfectly all right but was glad it was all over.

Her heart had screamed out one last cry of hope as his eyes had darkened as if he was angry she had said that and then he had kissed her. One last lingering kiss that was so poignantly final that her heart had given out its last cry of anguish. The barriers had shuttered then, like a prison door slamming for the last time on a lifer. And she was a lifer and would suffer forever more for the sentence she had brought about herself for loving him.

'Give me a few days to get things sorted out and I'll give you a call,' he'd said as he drew his lips from hers.

In other words, 'See you some time,' Justine thought achingly.

'Don't worry, I've masses to catch up on myself,' she tossed flippantly at him as she swung into the driver's seat of the Volvo.

She had taken one last painful look at his strapped arm and then through a blur of tears had accelerated out of his life.

'Justine, how many times must I repeat myself? He must have said something!' Teresa insisted.

Justine looked up from the food she couldn't eat and glared at her sister across the very same table that had started the decline in her life, the table she had sat at with Max, helping him with his food, feeling the pressure of his leg against hers, laughing with him when the meringue had taken a dive at his shirt-front.

'He said nothing, Teresa,' Justine told her heavily. 'He went over the mill with Greg Kendon and came back to the lodge exhausted. We didn't talk about it because he was in a hurry to get back.'

'But he must have given you some indication of which way he was going to swing.'

'He can swing by his neck from the highest tree for all I care,' Justine retorted and poured herself a hefty glass of claret.

'Typical of you, Justine. You can't take anything seriously in your absurd little life, can you?'

Too seriously, that's the trouble, Justine mused as she gulped her wine. She put the glass back down to the table and stared at it.

'If you want my honest opinion, Teresa,' Justine said quietly, 'I don't think there's a cat in hell's chance of Max Benedict giving his paper contract to Hammond's.'

There was a small silence and then Teresa pushed back her chair and stood up. She leaned on the table and looked menacingly across at her sister.

'Well, if he doesn't, Justine, it will be all your fault, and if Daddy's business collapses that will be all your fault too. For once in your life you had a chance to redeem yourself in this family and if you've blown it you'll have it on your conscience for the rest of your life.'

Fury swamped Justine then, fury and pain and the damned injustice of that! She stood up and faced her sister but she controlled her voice.

'I shall have nothing on my conscience, Teresa, because I've done *everything* you expected of me. I drove that one-armed bandit all over the country *en route* to Scotland, put up with his flights of fancy, satisfied his every whim, cut up his food for him, and yes, I did the other thing that was expected of me.'

Teresa stared at her in shocked disbelief. 'What... what do you mean?' she whispered.

'You know what I mean,' Justine cut back. What price pride now when she had nothing left? 'We were lovers on that trip,' she went on huskily and painfully, 'but whereas you expected a signed and sealed contract in return for your sister's services Max Benedict was cuter than all of us put together. The contract was never a consideration for him from the off. It was all a game to him and that's why we won't get the contract. He got what he wanted, a bit of fun, a bit of sport. He took one look at the mill and that salved his conscience for what he did to me. Once that was over it was, "Home, James, and don't spare the horses." He couldn't wait to ditch me. Yes, I'll suffer with my conscience for failing Daddy but you won't go unscathed, Teresa...' She stood tall and defiant against her sister, fighting the tears. 'You and your husband and your devious plans to get what you wanted for your own greed have caused me so... so much... pain... that one day... you might realise... might realise just what you've done... to me...'

She was sobbing now and in fury with herself for breaking down so easily she turned and rushed from the room, slamming the dining-room door hard behind her.

She would have to go, to get out of this house and away from the family. Soon Richard and her father would be back and she would have to face them with another failure and what on earth would happen to the company now?

'Open the door, Justine,' Teresa pleaded.

Wearily Justine rolled off the bed. She'd cried herself senseless, the first time since she had realised Max had used her so. It hadn't helped. She felt worse than ever.

Teresa stood in the doorway with a tray of coffee in her hands. She looked as drained as Justine felt. Justine stepped back to let her in, thinking that for Teresa to have carried that tray up from the kitchen must mean she felt some pity for her and maybe a bit guilty for what had happened.

'You're in love with him, aren't you?' Teresa murmured as she sat on the edge of the bed and poured the coffee for them.

Justine coiled on the bed next to her sister. 'It's that obvious, is it?'

Teresa nodded and handed her a cup of steaming coffee. 'I never for a moment thought it would get this far out of hand,' she started mournfully. 'I know we've had our differences but you are still my sister, Justine. I feel bad about it all.'

'Don't,' Justine assured her quietly. 'It wasn't your fault. I was the fool to have lost my heart and let my defences down.'

Teresa sighed heavily then. 'Are you sure he ditched you? I mean he's a busy man——'

'He ditched me,' Justine butted in. 'He didn't say the words but I knew.'

Teresa stirred her coffee thoughtfully. 'I wouldn't have had that happen for the world, and frankly I wouldn't have thought Max to be that hard and unfeeling. Still,' she gave a small shrug, 'you never know with people.'

They sipped their coffees pondering that thought and then Teresa went on earnestly, 'Honestly, Justine, I'm worried sick about the company. Richard has tried so hard and now with this baby coming... I couldn't bear to leave this house, I couldn't bear to see Daddy lose a lifetime's work. I only did what I thought was best——'

'Yes, for yourself,' Justine said flatly, though she thought that was unfair of her but she was so knotted up with grief she couldn't help feeling the worst of everyone concerned. If Teresa and Richard hadn't organised that wretched dinner party none of this would have happened.

Teresa sighed again. 'Yes, it's true,' she admitted. 'But I'm not like you. I need my security and I can see it slipping away from me. I love this house and I want to bring my children up here and I can't bear to think I won't be able to do that if the company goes. I never could understand you ever leaving it to travel the way you did. You know,

I hate to admit it, but in a way I was glad your business failed. That sounds terrible, I know, but I wanted you to fail because if you had succeeded then it would have made me feel even more inadequate. You're so much stronger than I am and I always envied you that independence, something I could never have done. I needed Daddy more than you, felt that I needed to prove myself all the time. I suppose that stemmed from Mother leaving...no, don't cry any more, Justine. I never meant to hurt you. I just thought...well, I knew that Max was interested in you——'

'He never was,' Justine sniffed mournfully. 'You saw with your own eyes his rejection of me at that launch.'

'He might have rejected you for any manner of reasons, Justine. It was his launch and he was frantically busy and he probably just didn't have time for you, but the interest was there. I saw it in his eyes and I wasn't wrong about that, and then when Richard mentioned you would be here at the dinner party——'

'You thought he would fall madly in love with me and would give Hammond's the contract.'

Teresa balanced her coffee-cup on her lap and rubbed her forehead fretfully. 'I don't know what I thought,' she admitted softly. 'I was so desperate to do something for Daddy, and Richard, and myself.' She shook her head in despair. 'I never thought it would work out like this, that you would be so affected, so hurt by all this.'

'Well, I am hurt, Teresa,' she whispered painfully. 'It hurts like hell to love someone who doesn't love you in return.'

They drank their coffee in silence and in her heart Justine knew she had to forgive her sister for everything because her own feelings about Max Benedict were small fry compared to the disaster that was about to happen to the company. She knew about failure only too well. Her father wouldn't be able to take this blow. Teresa and Richard would fare better. Like her, they would have to pick themselves up and carry on. But Justine knew how hard that would be for them. Her sister, in spite of her abrasiveness and her cruelty at times, was terrified of losing her status and that wasn't her fault. She was just made that way and couldn't change if she wanted to.

They were so very different. A weak sister and a strong one who could take the knocks of life and live with them. And Justine would have to live with those knocks, again and again.

'Tell me, Justine,' Teresa murmured and reached out to take her sister's hand. Her eyes were swimming with tears of regret. 'Did...did you start out by sleeping with Max because of that contract?'

Justine shook her head and lowered her lashes and her own tears spilled on to their clasped hands. 'No, Teresa, never that. I could never have done that, not for you or Daddy or the company, and it has nothing to do with not loving you enough. I do love you all and I care but I couldn't have done it for that.' She took a deep breath of recovery and lifted her face to look at her sister. 'I did it because I was so in love with him that it was inevitable. I fell for him four years ago. I loved him then and I love him now and I'll love him tomorrow.'

As she lay in bed later that night, Justine made a resolution. Though it would be desperately hard she could try and live without Max Benedict but she couldn't live with having failed the family business so something must be done about it. And tomorrow, she vowed, she would try and she would succeed this time. She must.

'I'm sorry but Mr Benedict is frightfully busy and couldn't possibly see you without an appointment,' 'sweetheart' informed her as Justine nervously stood before her in Max's outer office.

Justine recognised her as the same secretary she had confronted a few months before but mercifully 'sweetheart' didn't have such recall. She didn't look at all like a 'sweetheart', she was definitely a very efficient Lorna, highly trained in deflecting unwanted visitors from Max's inner sanctum.

Justine had decided that his home wasn't the place to tackle him, though his office could hardly be described as neutral ground but it was the only other alternative. And she had dressed accordingly in a taupe fine wool suit and a silk shirt she had sneaked out of Teresa's wardrobe without her knowing. She hadn't told her sister her intention to call on Max, not because she expected defeat and didn't want to disappoint her but more because she felt that Teresa would try to stop her. Her sister's repentance had touched her and they were closer now than they had ever been.

'Well, I'm sorry, but I'm *frightfully busy* too so could you please allow me to see him?'

'I'm sorry but that is not possible. Perhaps I can help.' She picked up a pen and a pad and looked up at Justine and her eyes narrowed. 'Haven't we met before?'

Justine wondered if it had been her job to clear up the poor little potted African violet. She coloured slightly at the thought. If she told her her name, the game would be up and she'd never get into see Max.

'I represent Hammond Paper and——' Oh, dear, a big mistake in mentioning the name Hammond. She wasn't doing very well at all.

Lorna's face hardened. 'I do remember you!'

Justine made a quick decision then after weighing up two choices. She could either front this strongly and decisively or crawl out of here with her tail between her legs. No choice really.

'Yes, well, it's not every day someone hurls a potted plant at your boss's head and if I don't get to see him, and now, I might go crazy again and do something even more *frightful*!'

'There is absolutely no need for that!' Lorna protested haughtily.

'Absolutely,' Justine retorted and headed straight for Max's office.

'You can't!'

Justine did. She swung open the door and stopped dead in her tracks.

'Justine!' Max exclaimed, turning towards the door as it burst open.

No exclamation came from Beverley's lips. She just stood next to Max with her hand lightly resting on his strapped arm as if it was the most natural thing in the world to do. But her eyes betrayed her, they narrowed in surprise as if Justine Hammond had no right in Max Benedict's office or anywhere else in his life.

In that instant Justine wanted to lurch across the room and claim that arm for her own. The arm she had prayed for, had kissed so tenderly, willing strength into. It was her arm to be worried about and cared for and adored, not Beverley's or any other woman's come to that.

But she had no claim, she reminded herself painfully.

'I'm sorry, Max, she just burst in. I couldn't stop her.'

The voice came from behind her and then Max spoke. 'It's all right, Lorna. I was expecting Justine. Beverley is just leaving. Would you show her out for me, please?'

Beverley's fingers curled possessively on his arm for a fraction of a second and then with great bravado she tilted her head up and kissed Max lightly on the cheek.

'See you soon, darling,' she breathed sexily and then with one final caress of his arm she turned and as she passed Justine she gave her a look that spoke volumes. Justine mentally put it into words. 'You haven't a ghost of a chance'.

Once they were alone Justine didn't know what to say because she hadn't expected to find Beverley with him. Not after all he had said about their relationship. She had actually believed him when he had claimed they were just good friends. She had trusted and believed and loved this man and what a fool she had been.

She found her voice at last. 'I expect you're wondering why I'm here.' The tone of her voice halted him in his tracks. He was actually coming across the wide expanse of dark blue Wilton to her and she wondered what his intention was. To pull her against him and say how wonderful it was to see her? Hardly. He'd made it obvious he wouldn't be bothered if he didn't see her ever again.

'Perhaps the same reason Beverley dropped in,' he suggested coolly.

'No, not that, Max,' she said drily.

'No, not what?'

'Not what you think.'

'So you *don't* want to wish me well for my operation.' A dark brow went up awaiting her answer and there was mockery in his eyes along with it.

Was she expected to believe that, that Beverley had dropped in with her good wishes and nothing else?

'Of course I wish you well for your operation,' she told him flatly. 'But you don't need my good wishes. You seem to be doing well enough already. I expect they'll be queuing up outside the hospital when it happens, like they do for a royal birth. No, I didn't especially come for that. I came to persuade you to rethink your decision not to give Hammond's your paper contract.'

There was a long silence in which neither of them spoke. He held the coldness of her eyes and Justine thought that she must have taken him by surprise. He probably thought she was here because she couldn't wait to see him again.

'Did your brother-in-law send you?' he asked icily.

'No, nor my sister or my father. I came of my own free will because I don't see why you should get away with ruining my family. And you will ruin it if you don't give us the contract. Do you realise——?'

'Just a minute,' he grated, eyes icy blue now. 'I don't want to hear some sob story——'

'You're not getting one, Max,' she interrupted equally coldly. 'You know damn well our product is top notch but you're not even willing to talk terms with my father——'

'Your father isn't even in the country to talk terms with, Justine. And, to repeat a well used phrase of yours, I don't waste time with the monkey when it's the organ grinder I want.'

'Don't try and be funny with me,' she lashed back furiously. 'You have no intention of discussing this with my father other than to tell him you don't want his paper. You never were interested. All you wanted was...'

'Yes, Justine, what exactly did I want?' he grazed wickedly, the very narrowing of his eyes daring her to answer.

She bit her lip as her voice trapped in her throat. She couldn't even say it, that he had wanted her, just for fun, and when that fun began to sour he couldn't wait to be rid of her. It would be too painful to verbalise what she knew in her heart.

'I didn't come here to discuss personal issues. I came——'

'Well, it's a pity you didn't,' he growled. 'Because I would have thought more of you if you had shown a bit of warmth. Now, listen good and hard, Justine, because I get mad when I have to repeat myself. My business affairs have nothing to do with you——'

'They have when they concern my family's business. I drove you all the way to Scotland for one purpose and one purpose only...' as she was saying it she knew it was coming out all wrong but it was too late to rectify it '... your paper contract. You need good-quality paper and we supply it. There is absolutely no reason for you not to take us up. We are a small, independent company that will give you superlative service, a service you won't get from the conglomerates. You need us, Max Benedict, and costings and terms are easily resolved. We are the best and you expect the best so there is absolutely no excuse for you not to give us your business.'

'Have you quite finished?'

Breathless she stared at him, so terribly unsure now. She saw anger now in his eyes and he was trying so hard to clench his injured hand against his chest. He was furious and she had seen that fury before but somehow, in his beautifully cut navy suit and crisp white shirt it intensified the depth of it, making him look frighteningly formidable. And yet Justine still felt that magnetism towards him, that half-crazy thrill of brushing with danger when she pushed him hard enough.

'No, I haven't finished,' she told him in a very soft voice. If nothing else worked she would use emotional blackmail on him as he had used it on her to get her to take that trip with him.

'Go on,' he rasped, still angry, still tense.

Justine swallowed hard. 'A few months back I needed you but you rejected my work. I'll get over that and live to fight another day. I need you now because my father will lose a lifetime's work if he doesn't get your contract and he won't live to fight another day if you fail him. You once said you were all for free enterprise—well, my father has fought to keep the company a private one, a family business. So I'm pleading on his behalf now for you to reconsider.'

He took a long long time to come back with anything to her plea. He just stood watching her, still angry, still tense. At last he spoke, his voice deep with an emotion Justine didn't understand.

'Were you preparing that pretty little speech in your mind when we were making love, Justine? Did you sleep with me for my contract?'

The very question her own sister had asked. Then she had answered it truthfully, but how could she blurt the truth to this man, that she had loved him before he was even aware of her existence, that she had heaved that potted plant at his head because she had been so stricken with his indifference to her that she had wanted to punish him for that cold rejection? And she wanted to punish again, a last desperate punishment to leave him with.

'Wasn't that what was expected of me?' she breathed, and as she said it she thought that it wasn't a very harsh punishment because for it to strike home he would have had to care in the first place.

'That isn't an answer,' he said bitterly.

'I'm afraid it's all you're going to get, because I didn't come here to rake up what happened between us on the way to Scotland. I came to plead my father's case and——'

'And that is answer enough for me, Justine,' he stated coldly and flatly. 'Now if you'll excuse me I'm——'

'Frightfully busy,' she finished for him, desperately feeling defeat swooping down on her from a great height—yet again. She stepped towards him, not even sure of what she was going to do or say, but she couldn't let him dismiss her for a third time without a fight. 'You weren't frightfully busy last week. You had time on your *one good hand* then to give me your attention. But then you had a motive, didn't you? You accuse me of having a motive for loving you but what was yours, Max Benedict? I'll tell you because you can't be trusted to speak the truth. You used me, as you use all your women, no doubt. The object of the exercise was to seduce me, which you did, and the least you can do is pay for that.'

'Corporate prostitution,' he growled, stepping dangerously close to her. 'Well, let me tell you I've never had to pay for it in my life, in or out of business, and if you think you've done your father any favours by acting like a mercenary little . . .' His lips thinned as if he couldn't bring himself to utter the word that was perilously hanging on his lips.

'Say no more,' she husked defiantly, terribly hurt by that, but hadn't she asked for it? 'I know exactly what you think of me. But you don't come out of this squeaky-clean either, Max. I despise you as much as you despise me and——'

To her utter humiliation he caught her unawares. In one sharp movement he had her by the waist with that good arm of his which seemed even more dangerously powerful than before. His lips met hers in a crushing blow that nearly knocked her senseless but the most shocking thing about it was that it powered such a deep, deep love for him that she wondered at her sanity.

He continued to kiss her, long and painfully, till she wanted to scoop her arms around his neck and tell him the whole truth, the truth she had only just realised. She hadn't come here for her father or her sister or that damned contract of his. She had come for herself, to see him one more time in the hope that he might realise that he loved her and wanted her and couldn't live without her.

Teenage dreams? She had never outgrown them. So now she knew what she was going to do with the rest of her life. She was going to grow up.

He released her at last and she stepped back and gazed up at him with tears in her eyes. Her fists hung clenched at her sides and her whole body was stiff with tension for this great loss in her life.

Her words came stilted with passion and a heated response to that last punishing blow of his. 'This . . . will be your loss . . . not mine, Max,' she croaked defiantly in a last bid to somehow get back at him.

He raised a mocking dark brow. 'I'm experiencing a touch of *déjà vu*, I believe. Forget any ideas of hurling another pot at my head, Justine, because I learn quickly. You'll never catch me unawares again,' he told her ominously. 'Now get out before I take that kiss a stage further and show you exactly what you did come here for.'

Shocked, she took another step back. Did he know? Justine stared at him, trying to analyse that fierce look in his eyes. Yes, he knew, and shame and humiliation hit her. She could do nothing right in her life. Not for herself or the man she loved or her family. She was an utter failure at everything.

She turned and walked to the door and if there had been a potted violet to hand she wouldn't have bothered throwing it. She had neither the strength nor the will.

CHAPTER NINE

'OH, I'M exhausted,' Teresa sighed as Justine pulled into the gates of the manor. 'Shopping drains you, doesn't it?'

'Hmm,' was all Justine could muster, just as exhausted as her sister. What had started out as a good idea to get out from under Richard's and their father's feet had turned out to be a painful experience for Justine though she had kept her spirits up for the sake of Teresa. Shopping for baby clothes and nursery equipment in London a couple of weeks before Christmas wasn't to be advised. And definitely not to be advised for anyone suffering with a broken heart as Justine was.

Teresa had been in her element in the baby departments of numerous stores but Justine had experienced something she had never thought she was capable of—envy. The baby clothes had been so beautiful and she had touched them and enthused with her sister, but her heart wasn't in it. She imagined what it must be like to be carrying the child of the man you loved so deeply, to be planning a nursery and choosing names and the ache of knowing it would never happen for her was miserable.

'Whose car's that?' Teresa queried as the headlights picked out a Jaguar parked on the driveway.

Justine nearly slammed on the brakes of the Volvo with shock. She knew that car. Max was here. Her heart started to thud dangerously. He had obviously come to give his decision on the paper contract personally.

And Justine knew what that decision would be and her heart died a little for what her father must be hearing now because it would be bad news. Since storming Max's office she had had time to regret ever going near him again. She had made it ten times worse. Max Benedict *might* have been considering giving them the contract but after that disastrous meeting she had hopelessly made a mess of it would be a definite no, no.

'It's Max's car,' Justine told her as she pulled up outside the garage block.

'Good news, maybe?' Teresa suggested tentatively.

'I doubt Max Benedict knows how to deliver good news and I hardly think he's here to wish us all a merry Christmas either,' Justine said dolefully as she collected the packages off the back seat. 'You go in, Teresa, I'll bring all this stuff in.'

Teresa couldn't wait to get inside the house to find out what her future was, though Justine ruefully reflected that her future had hardly been a consideration on their shopping trip. Teresa had spent as if there was no tomorrow.

Justine didn't go into the front entrance after Teresa. She skirted the manor and went into the kitchen from the back door because if there was a chauffeur sitting in the kitchen with Janet she wouldn't have to suffer the indignity of facing the alternative chauffeur, Beverley.

Justine was dismayed to find no one in the kitchen. That meant...she didn't know what it meant so she hurried through and straight up to her bedroom, only pausing in the hallway to listen out for voices. She heard deep mumbles coming from the study, mainly her father and Richard, and, not wanting to suffer the agony of hearing Max's voice, she hurried on upstairs.

'It's not Max's car,' Teresa told her as she came out of the bathroom on the landing.

'But I'd know that car anywhere,' Justine protested. 'I've driven it!'

Teresa frowned. 'Well, Greg Kendon's driving it now.'

Justine had forgotten the arrangement Max had made with Greg and she quickly explained it to her sister, feeling half relieved and half disappointed that Max wasn't here in the house.

Teresa looked affronted. 'Bit much, that, Greg driving his swish car around as if it was his own.' She shrugged. 'There was I thinking that that's where the company profits were going, into the pocket of the works manager. That car must be worth a small fortune. Come on, let's go and gloat over the baby stuff.'

Justine followed her into her and Richard's bedroom and dumped the packages on the bed. 'You gloat; it's your baby. I'm off for a well-earned bath before dinner. I'll come and gloat later.'

Justine locked the bathroom door after her and leaned wearily back against it to settle her thoughts.

Yes, she was disappointed Max wasn't here because deep down she still nurtured the hope that he might come after her. A hopeless hope, though. He wouldn't come because he didn't care and he never had.

Seeing that car parked outside had brought the trip flooding back to her and reminded her that she had no idea when his operation was going to be, and she wanted to know so much because even if she wasn't a part of his life any more she cared deeply enough to want to know the outcome. But she had no contact, no one she could ring and ask, however unobtrusively. The thought heightened her isolation and her loss.

As she ran the bath she switched her thoughts to Greg. Had Max sent him with the bad news rather than come here himself and possibly face her again? Or was Greg just free-wheeling around in Max's car till it was time to deliver it back? Neither supposition carried much weight and as Justine wearily shed her clothes she decided it didn't much matter anyway. What did matter though was the company problems and she couldn't imagine how her father could carry on now.

Later when she went downstairs she was astounded to hear what sounded like a champagne cork being popped and excited voices coming from the drawing-room, mainly the excited voices of Richard and Teresa, who sounded in a celebratory mood; her father was a more sombre person, not the sort to show his emotions so openly.

As Justine stepped into the room her first impression was of the change in her father. When he had returned from Brussels with Richard yesterday he had looked an old man; now the transformation in him was remarkable. He looked years younger and had a sparkle in his eyes she hadn't seen for so long and Justine wondered . . .

Her heart hammered as she went to her father's side. 'What are we celebrating?'

Her father hugged her. 'A reprieve, Justine, and we have you to thank for it. If you hadn't offered to drive Max Benedict to Scotland to look over the mill we'd have nothing to celebrate now.'

So Max had capitulated and the contract was Hammond's'. Justine wasn't sure how she felt about that. She should feel elated for the family and the company and part of her was, but a part of her felt a great shame for her own part in getting this deal.

Justine and Teresa exchanged glances and Justine felt assured that Teresa hadn't revealed the truth to her father and Richard, that she had paid for this contract: an emotional price that far outweighed the value of the contract itself.

'So...so you got the contract,' Justine murmured, taking a glass of champagne from her father. Her plea had worked and she had stabbed at Max's conscience and she should feel happy that it had worked but she didn't. It all left a horribly sour taste in the mouth.

'More than the contract, Justine. Max wants a partnership with Hammond's,' Richard told her promptly as if he personally had scooped the business deal of the decade.

Justine's hand tightened around the stem of her glass. Inside she felt as chilled as the champagne but no bubbles fizzed with excitement around her heart. She could see what the others couldn't, that Max Benedict was a ruthless scheming rat and was unmercifully cruel in how he used people.

'My God,' she breathed, looking at all of them in turn. 'You can't see the wood for the trees, can you?'

All eyes were suddenly upon her, her father's particularly astonished that she was voicing an opinion on something she had never taken an interest in before.

'He's blackmailed you into that partnership,' she went on heatedly. 'No deal, no contract. A partnership today and tomorrow he'll want full control and you'll all be out with his boot behind you. It will be the finish of Hammond's if you go through with this deal——'

'Justine,' Richard grated impatiently. 'You really don't know anything of these matters.'

'I know that Max Benedict doesn't do anything without gain for himself,' she retaliated bitterly. She should know. He had used her and now he was punishing her for having the audacity to plead Hammond's case. No doubt that disastrous meeting had inspired him with revenge. Yes, why not give poor ailing Hammond Paper his contract and have a last stab at her by taking it over completely?

'I never knew you took such an interest in the family business, Justine,' John Hammond said to his daughter.

'It's a recent thing,' Justine told him. Since falling in love with a one-armed bandit who robbed hearts and companies.

'Then you must understand that Richard and I know what we're doing,' her father went on brusquely. 'Max has already stated his terms, which we are completely in agreement with. He wants to put money into the business because he can see the potential for expansion. He was very impressed with what he saw in Scotland. He had long talks with Greg and because we were away and he would be incapacitated in hospital he asked Greg to bring his proposals to us to discuss...'

There was more, mostly benefits to the company, but Justine only half listened. What was singing in her ears was that Max had talked this over with Greg, days ago in Scotland. *Before* she had pleaded her case, *before* he had dropped her out of his life.

Justine sipped her champagne thoughtfully and moved away from Richard and her father, who were carrying on a conversation way above her and Teresa's head. Teresa joined her by the window and together they gazed out into a clear and frosty night.

'If Max Benedict doesn't care a jot for you, Justine, he's got a funny way of showing it,' Teresa said in a low voice.

'It's a business deal,' Justine told her grumpily.

'He didn't have to take it as far as a partnership.'

'It's still a business deal and a stab in the back for me.'

'*If* what you say is true and he used you and ditched you, why should he want to hurt you further? It doesn't make sense.' Teresa looked meaningfully at her sister and then gave a slow smile. 'If you ask me, he's crazy about you and this is one way of keeping you in his life, by binding himself into your father's company. Sure, it's a good business deal for all involved, but if he hated the sight of you, which you only suppose, he'd hardly be doing this. He'd do the reverse, put his business elsewhere and so put you out of his life forever.'

Such words of wisdom from her sister and oh, how she wanted to believe them. But he had ditched her, more or less. He hadn't exactly said, though, so could she have jumped to all sorts of depressing conclusions since their last night in Scotland? But there was no explanation for his sudden coldness to her after leaving the mill but . . . but he had made love to her that night before they had left and. . . and there had been reasons for his sudden bouts of moodiness on that trip—his injured arm.

Had the anticipation of a negative outcome of his operation put him off making a commitment to her? Was he afraid she would reject him if it wasn't successful and he had to live with a useless arm? He'd said he felt confident about it but was that just a cover up for his real feelings?

'Oh, I wish . . .' Justine murmured softly.

'Wish what?'

'Wish that I knew when Max was being operated on,' she said mournfully because if she knew it would be an excuse to go and see him and perhaps find out the truth for herself.

'Tomorrow morning,' Teresa told her with a small smile. 'At the Ascot Palmer Clinic, ten o'clock in the morning.'

Justine didn't even ask her how she knew because she was wallowing in that knowledge and there was a warm feeling swishing through her and giving her a small flame to feed on.

She took her and Teresa's empty glasses, refilled them both and took them back to the window where her sister was still standing, gently smoothing a hand over the slight bump in her stomach and looking dreamily out into the floodlit winter gardens.

'Here's to the first Hammond baby,' Justine said and together they raised their glasses and Justine added a silent toast of her own to that. And here's to 'the poor baby' himself, the one who didn't need her good wishes to come out of this operation because everything was going to be all right. She felt it in her bones.

'He's not conscious yet,' the sister told her outside Max's room. 'But you're welcome to go and gaze at him for five minutes.' Her eyes sparkled mischievously. 'We do, and it's not because we have to. He's drop-dead gorgeous even when he's unconscious.'

Justine grinned and stepped into the room. She shut the door quietly behind her and tiptoed across to his bedside.

The room was full of flowers, expensive orchids and waxy lilies, bowls and vases of roses from well-wishers. Justine cynically supposed they were all from women.

Gingerly she shifted some aside and put her own offering, a tiny pot of African violets, on the table by the window so that he would see them as soon as he opened his eyes. There was a chance he'd want to sink back into unconsciousness at the sight of them but in her heart she knew he wouldn't because she'd thought long and hard about that trip to Scotland. She'd relived those moments of pure heady sensation when they had loved so deeply. She couldn't, she just couldn't disregard them. They had happened, they had been real and somehow she had lost sight of them along the way.

She stood by his bedside and gazed down at him. He looked so peaceful as he recovered. His hair was endearingly tousled at his brow and he had such long thick black lashes that no one would believe his eyes were so blue beneath. His mouth was perfectly relaxed and she wanted to touch his lips with her fingertips but she was afraid he would wake up and she didn't want that. She had purposely picked her time knowing he would still be sleeping off the anaesthetic. She wasn't a coward, but she knew it wasn't the time or the place for resolving this with whys and wherefores. She just wanted to be here with him for a few minutes.

His right arm lay heavily bandaged at his side. She hadn't asked the sister if the operation had been a success because she didn't have to. She knew it was because he had known it would be. She bent down and lovingly grazed a kiss across his brow. She loved him so much and when he woke up he would feel that kiss on his brow and he would know.

Justine tiptoed back to the table and gazed at the most impressive display of red roses that had been delivered from Interflora. She read the card unflinchingly. It was gushing and sentimental and was from Beverley and because it was a telephoned order the card wasn't written in her own handwriting.

Justine took a pen and a small notepad from her shoulder bag and started to write. At least Max would know she had been here personally and would know that she really cared though it wasn't in her nature to be gushing and sentimental.

I would have heaved this at your head
but you were already out cold.

She wrote and signed it, with love from 'the driver'.

She kissed the note and then tucked it into the plant and, taking one last look at the man she adored, she smiled and left the room.

Four days later Justine and Teresa were in the drawing-room decorating the Christmas tree after tea. Already Justine had clumsily broken three of the delicate glass baubles as she unpacked them. Her nerves were shot to pieces because she had waited and waited and hoped and prayed and not one word had come from Max. She had crashed blindly through every emotion since her visit to the hospital and was now in a state of total despair. The operation hadn't been a success.... It had been a success... He just didn't care for her... He didn't want her... He did want her but...

She didn't know any more, didn't know anything and couldn't ask her father or Richard if they knew how he was, and she hadn't the nerve to phone the clinic and Teresa wasn't saying anything because she had witnessed all those emotions and was as scared as her sister.

Janet put her head round the door. 'Phone for you, Justine. Where do you want to take it?'

Justine glanced nervously at her sister.

'Who is it, Janet?'

'He wouldn't give his name,' came the reply.

'Well, it can only be *him*,' Teresa cried excitedly.

Justine was frozen to the spot and then Teresa gave her a push and she reeled to the door to take the call in the hall.

'Hello,' she murmured, her heart racing so hard in her ears that she doubted she'd hear anything but that thud, thud.

'I need a driver and my chauffeur is off duty. Can you help?' he appealed in a low, low voice.

'W-where are you?' She thought he must still be at the hospital with no one to drive him home. Where were all those so-called well-wishers when he needed them?

'I'm at home,' he told her.

Her heart stopped. Oh, dear God. The operation had been a failure. He'd never drive again. But at least he had called her and not Beverley. But maybe he already had and she was unavailable and Justine was his second choice!

In a very fragile voice she asked, 'Where do you want to go?'

'Does it matter?'

Justine pulled herself together. He sounded low, as if he had a bad case of the blues. Post-operative blues, a million times worse if the operation had been fruitless. He needed her. That was why he had rung her. *He needed her.*

'Yes, it matters,' she said brightly. 'If it's a long trip I need to pack and arrange the route and this time I call the shots, Max Benedict.'

She heard his soft laughter down the phone and her heart soared. 'I already know the route and a toothbrush will suffice. I'll see you in an hour.' The line went dead and she stared at the receiver stupidly before slipping it back into place.

'Well!' Teresa cried when she went back into the drawing-room, Justine so bemused she didn't know what to think.

Justine shrugged and looked helplessly at her sister. 'I don't know. He's at home and he said he needed a chauffeur and could I help and he wants me in an hour.' She raked her hair from her forehead. 'Oh, Teresa, if he needs a driver his arm can't be——'

'Don't be silly, Justine. He can only just be out of hospital. He's probably still all stitched up and in pain——'

'And he needs me,' Justine sighed, closing her eyes. 'And it doesn't matter about his arm and I'll tell him that it makes no difference to me and I'll convince him that it shouldn't matter to him because I love him and I'll do everything for him and he need never worry again and——'

'My God. I'd say he needs you in that mood as badly as he needs his other arm in plaster,' Teresa teased. 'Leave the poor man with just a little pride, Justine.'

Justine reflected on that as she hurried to change into the violet silk dress that was getting yet another airing. She mustn't overdo the sympathy attitude. She could smother him out of her life at this rate. He hated fuss, but only when it didn't suit him.

Later she pulled up outside his mansion and sat in the car to compose herself before going in. It suddenly occurred to her that he needed her to drive him to some swish restaurant where he was going to meet Beverley or some other dreaded female who would no doubt relish cutting up his food for him... Was she going crazy again? Max Benedict couldn't be that cruel! No he needed her, only her in his life, and she would drive him to the ends of the earth to hear that.

He was waiting at the open door when she ran up the steps. The first thing she looked at was his right arm still strapped to his chest and her heart bleeped miserably to see that nothing had changed. But maybe there was a change for her in his eyes, a warmth and a love at the sight of her rushing to him. She supposed it was too much to ask as he looked at her so unemotionally, his eyes so blue and intense but sadly lacking what she so longed to see.

He didn't say a word as he stepped back from the doorway for her to enter. He didn't look as if only days before he had been through surgery. He was dressed in a beautiful evening suit, dressed ready to dine in a swish restaurant somewhere. Her pulses dulled at the thought that he had indeed summoned her just for her chauffeuring abilities.

He showed her into the drawing-room where once, a lifetime ago, they had pored over the route map, planning the trip. It was there he had appreciated her perfume, teased her and made his ridiculous demands. Yes, she had lived a lifetime since then, and she'd sacrifice another lifetime if they could go back and do it all over again.

A fire blazed in the grate where no fire had blazed that late afternoon when they had set off for Bath. She stared at the glow of the coals and didn't know what to say, and he wasn't helping by staying so silent. She slid out of her coat and she felt him behind her, taking the coat from her arms. She looked up at the marble mantelpiece and her potted African violet held centre stage and the thought rushed at her that he had cared enough to bring it home with him.

She swung and faced him and her cheeks were flushed and the words ran like a rippling stream from her lips.

'I had a terrible time finding an African violet before Christmas. The shops are full of Poinsettias . . . and . . . and chrysanthemums. And Christmas trees and holly of course . . . after all it's nearly Christmas . . . but I found one and——'

He was half smiling at the rush of her words and she felt an idiot and she thought this was just the time when he should be taking her in his arm and telling her he loved her. But he didn't. He just stood smiling down at her and making no attempt to ease her misery.

Her eyes settled on his strapped arm and then she looked up at him and asked tentatively, 'H-how is it?'

He held her eyes briefly before turning away but didn't answer her query. 'What would you like to drink?'

Her insides seized. He didn't want to talk about it so it was bad news.

'Nothing,' she said quietly. 'I don't drink and drive.'

'We're not going anywhere,' he told her calmly and walked to a drinks table and poured two glasses of brandy.

She watched him, shifting uncomfortably, wondering why she was here if they weren't going anywhere. But there must be a reason and maybe it was because he had changed his mind about the contract with Hammond's and wanted her to deliver the news to her father and Richard. It spurred sharp words to her lips.

'So why am I here? Why did you summon me if you don't need me to drive you anywhere? If it's anything to do with your wicked plan to take over my father's business then you can forget it. I'm not open to emotional blackmail——'

'Were you ever?' he asked darkly as he came back to her to hand her a glass of brandy.

She took it though she had no intention of drinking it. She had come here with hope in her heart but it didn't seem as though he had summoned her here with the same illusions. He went back to the table for his own glass which further enforced on her stretched emotions that he hadn't got the use of his injured arm back.

'Can I sit down?' she murmured, feeling decidedly shaky now.

He nodded to the sofa and she slumped into it and he stood by the fireplace looking down on her.

'I asked you a question,' he said.

'Was I ever open to emotional blackmail?' she repeated dolefully and then she did take a sip of brandy because she needed it now. 'Why...why are you asking me that?'

'Because you didn't give me a good enough answer the last time I asked you.'

'You never have asked me before, not directly. The last time we spoke you asked me if I'd slept with you for my father's contract. Is that what you mean? Is that what you're asking me again now?'

'More or less, and I'd like a straight answer this time, not an evasive "wasn't that what was expected of me?". I'd also like you to look at me instead of burying your face in that brandy glass.'

She looked up at him though it made her neck ache to meet his gaze. Her heart ached too because she wondered what the point of all this was. It seemed to be some sort of slow torture he was putting her through. She was hurt to think he thought that she'd slept with him for that wretched contract, and when she was hurt she fired back the only way she knew to relieve the pain.

'The very question is contemptible and says nothing for you for even considering asking it but nothing surprises you about me.'

'Well, perhaps this comes as a surprise to you. I've been eaten up with fear, the fear that you just might have slept with me for that bloody contract. It's been gnawing away at me like this pain in my arm. When you came to my office I thought you'd come for any other reason but to plead your father's case.'

She stared at him, trying to unravel what he had just suggested but it was so hard to understand when she was feeling so confused.

'And I suppose you think those violets were left at your bedside as a thank-you for what you think you've done for Hammond Paper. You really are a cold bastard, Max.'

She stood up and slammed her brandy glass on the mantelpiece next to him and gripped the edge of the marble to steady herself. 'And for your further information I'm not overjoyed about your condescending attitude to my family's business, though the others are cock-a-hoop about it, but then they don't know you the way I do. You're like a plate-glass window to me, I can see right through you. Your paper contract and a partnership today and tomorrow Hammond Paper won't exist. You want the lot——'

He gripped the wrist that was hanging on to the mantelpiece. 'I want *you*, Justine, and if you can't see that through the plate-glass window of my soul you need your eyes tested.'

'What?' she cried, so taken by surprise she didn't even struggle out of his heated grasp.

'Yes, what! What does it take to get you to open up your heart and speak some good honest truths?'

She stared at him in disbelief. 'Truth!' she squawked. 'That's good coming from you—you can't even spell the word. I don't tell lies. I'm not clever enough. I'm a damned open book about the way I feel about you.'

His grip tightened and his eyes were steely ice. 'Well, I don't read so well, so say it, then, Justine, say just how crazy you are about me and put both of us out of our misery.'

'M-misery? Well . . . yes . . . it would be a misery for me and jubilation for you if I opened up my heart,' she cried angrily. 'Then you'll have it all won't you? Simpering compliance from me and my father's company——'

'I don't care a damn about Hammond Paper or your father's feelings. I've made a very good business move and that's all there is to that. What I want in my personal life is you but I'm not prepared to put myself on the line before I hear from you that you want me!'

So inflamed, Justine missed the whole point of what he was trying to say. 'Oh, how damned childish can you get?' she stormed. 'You won't say you love me till I say I love you. Well, I won't, so there, so just you let me go and——'

She went to wrench her wrist from his, glaring at his fearful grasp as if to laser it away from her flesh. She stared in astonishment at his fingers gripping her tightly, then her eyes, wide and enormous, travelled from those fingers to his wrist, to his arm, to the leather strap lying loosely from his neck.

Max was gripping her with his injured arm, the arm he had led her to believe was as useless as it had been before the operation! He was all right! His arm was working perfectly! And...and he wanted her in his life!

'You...you...' And then she was in his arms, both of them, and she was clinging to him and mouthing hot kisses across his cheek. 'Oh, you make me so mad!' she cried.

'And you make me madder,' he grated against her hair and then his mouth was seeking hers and when their lips came together the clash was as fierce as their battles.

'Oh, I love you, Max Benedict,' she breathed when they drew apart for breath.

'Now, because you know my arm is better?' He was grinning down at her and she punched his chest.

'Yes, because your arm is better,' she repeated with laughter in her voice. 'You're unbearable with it strapped to your chest and no one in their right mind could love you that way.'

'Which means you're not in your right mind,' he teased.

'I am now,' she told him, though she was feeling decidedly dizzy with happiness.

'So you wouldn't have married me if the operation hadn't been a success?'

She knew in her heart that that wasn't a serious question and she had been a fool to think that his bad arm had ever been an issue between them.

'I won't marry you now it *has* been a success,' she teased. 'Not till you tell me that you love me.'

He pursed his lips. 'I don't know about that. Loving you could be a commitment that even I might balk at.'

'Coward,' she laughed.

'Yes, I am, Justine Hammond. You terrify the life out of me.'

'Because I throw things?'

'My reactions are sharp enough to get out of the way of flying violets but I'm not sure about damaging my heart.' He tightened his grip around her. 'I've never been in love before, you see——'

'So you *are* in love with me?' Her eyes were bright and waiting for those delicious words but would he ever get them out?

'I must be if I've asked you to marry me.'

'You haven't.'

'Oh, haven't I?'

'Not properly. You've hedged around it a bit but that isn't good enough for me. I want the full-blown proposal on bended knee.'

He grinned. 'No can do I'm afraid. Bit of cartilage trouble since my youth on the rugby pitch.'

'Strewth!' Justine exhaled. 'Am I to marry a cripple?'

'Only an emotional cripple. My heart's in traction waiting for your answer.'

She linked her arms around his neck and kissed his chin. 'And if I put you out of your misery and accept, will you tell me how much you love me?'

'You go first,' he teased. 'I want to hear it again and perhaps this will help you on your way.' He reached into his pocket and took out a small leatherbound box.

In astonishment Justine stepped back and stared at it with eyes, green and wide.

With his right hand he flicked open the box and her eyes were blinded by a huge solitaire diamond. She recognised it immediately.

'Max,' she cried and her eyes darted from the priceless gem to the priceless gems of his beautiful blue eyes. 'It's the ring from Chester,' she gasped. 'St Cedryche's ring!'

'I knew then I was hopelessly in love with you,' he explained quietly. 'In fact I began to fall when that potted plant was hurtling towards me and then I really fell badly at that awful dinner party of your brother-in-law's. I think it was the dreaded meringue that did it.'

Her eyes were swimming with tears of happiness as Max took the gorgeous ring from its velvety lair and slipped it on the third finger of her left hand. With his right hand he lifted the ring to his lips as if to bless it and their love forever more.

'Gosh,' she breathed in awe. 'It must have cost you an arm and a leg!'

'Can't you be serious for a moment?' he laughed.

She looked at him in surprise and then realised what she had said and grinned, her eyes sparkling as fiercely as the diamond on her finger.

'Oh, why, Max, why didn't you tell me before how you felt?'

'Simple. Fear, absolute total fear that you didn't feel the same way.'

'Oh, Max. I've loved you for so long, since Belgravia——'

'Belgravia!' he exclaimed, bringing a flush of embarrassment to her cheeks. She lowered her head and he lifted her chin to look into her eyes.

'Justine, are you serious?'

She nodded, biting her lip. 'You were the most fascinating man I'd ever seen in my life and when I cornered you by the potted ferns——'

'Potted azaleas,' he corrected with a gleam of mischief in his eyes.

She smiled. 'So you do remember?'

'Yes, though a lot of potted whatevers have hurled through the air since.'

'Only one, Max. You had rejected me a second time and I was so furious . . .' She shrugged. 'Well, you know.'

'Tell me, did you think I had rejected you a third time in Scotland?'

'Yes,' she breathed mournfully, meeting his pained gaze. 'Everything was so good before you went to the mill and then when you came back you were cold and tired and I thought you hadn't seen anything that pleased you and you wouldn't give the contract to my father and then I began to think that you were regretting our affair and wondering how you could get out of it.'

'No, not that,' Max murmured. 'I did rather find myself in a difficult situation. The mill was much smaller than I expected, productive but not productive enough for my needs. After talking with Greg I decided a partnership with your father was worth a try with a view to expansion and I was preoccupied with that when I got back to you. You were sleeping when I got back and I gazed down at you for so long, loving you and wanting you in my life and yet so very uncertain how you felt about me. I know we had shown our feelings to each other when we made love but I couldn't get out of my mind how we'd started out on that trip in the first place.'

'Pushed into it by my brother-in-law and my sister?'

'And manipulated by me to get what I wanted from you, your love, your compliance——'

'And my helping hand,' she finished for him in a loving whisper. She smiled and then frowned slightly. 'Max, did you consider that I wouldn't want you if...if the operation hadn't been a success?'

'I never had any doubt that it would be.'

'I did,' she admitted quietly. 'Lots of times, but it didn't alter how I felt about you. I knew I could cope but I often wondered if that was why you held back from me at times. You used to get so cross when I helped you and I knew you had your pride.'

'And my pain,' he told her. 'If I was moody it was because it ached so miserably at times and I just wanted this operation over with and to get on with my life. It was an inconvenience I didn't need.'

'But we would never have got together if it hadn't happened and we would never have got together if my father's business hadn't being going so badly.'

He gathered her hard into his arms and brushed his mouth over her hair. 'True, but life would have thrown us together in another way because we were meant for each other, Justine,' he murmured softly in her ear.

His lips moved from her hair to her face and then when they reached her own waiting lips he kissed her so passionately that it was all the confirmation she needed of how deeply he loved her.

Two arms enfolded her firmly into his need and for Justine it was a new exhilarating experience. A wonderful, exciting start to a new and wonderfully exciting life with this man who wasn't going to escape her a third time.

When at last he released her mouth she slowly slid the leather strap from around his neck. She smiled up at him as she tossed it carelessly aside.

'You were trawling for sympathy by wearing that tonight, weren't you?'

That very dextrous right hand of his slid seductively across her breast and Justine's desire spun her dizzily as an aching need for him rushed her senses.

'I always was an opportunist. If all else failed I would have thrown myself on your mercy.'

'And you might have had a certain African violet thrown at your head for your trouble.'

'You'll never have need to do that again, my darling, because I'll never make you that furious again, because I love you so very much.'

She took both his hands in hers and kissed them both tenderly in turn, relishing the warmth and the life in the hand that had given them both so much trouble. She knew then what she was going to do with the rest of her life. She was going to devote it to loving this man and bearing his children and growing African violets. Then she looked up into his eyes and said very quietly,

'If you truly love me and don't want to make me mad you'd better show me how a man with two hands makes love.'

He smiled and slid his hands out from hers and moved them round her waist to lower her to the sofa in front of the fire. Then he showed her just how much she had been missing by removing their clothes slowly and teasingly with two very able hands till she was soon murmuring her love and her need.

They loved till the fire in the grate dimmed to a dull glow, but the glow in their hearts was anything but dull. It flamed bright and clear with the promise of such joy and happiness to come and it would never dim and fade, because love like theirs had been fought for with a fury and won with a fury, and it was a victory to be savoured.

Next Month's Romances

Each month you can choose from a wide variety of romance with Mills & Boon. Below are the new titles to look out for next month, why not ask either Mills & Boon Reader Service or your Newsagent to reserve you a copy of the titles you want to buy – just tick the titles you would like and either post to Reader Service or take it to any Newsagent and ask them to order your books.

Please save me the following titles:	Please tick	✓
THE SULTAN'S FAVOURITE	Helen Brooks	
INFAMOUS BARGAIN	Daphne Clair	
A TRUSTING HEART	Helena Dawson	
MISSISSIPPI MOONLIGHT	Angela Devine	
TIGER EYES	Robyn Donald	
COVER STORY	Jane Donnelly	
LEAP OF FAITH	Rachel Elliot	
EVIDENCE OF SIN	Catherine George	
THE DAMARIS WOMAN	Grace Green	
LORD OF THE MANOR	Stephanie Howard	
INHERITANCE	Shirley Kemp	
PASSION'S PREY	Rebecca King	
DYING FOR YOU	Charlotte Lamb	
NORAH	Debbie Macomber	
PASSION BECOMES YOU	Michelle Reid	
SHADOW PLAY	Sally Wentworth	

If you would like to order these books in addition to your regular subscription from Mills & Boon Reader Service please send £1.90 per title to: Mills & Boon Reader Service, Freepost, P.O. Box 236, Croydon, Surrey, CR9 9EL, quote your Subscriber No:................................. (if applicable) and complete the name and address details below. Alternatively, these books are available from many local Newsagents including W H Smith, J Menzies, Martins and other paperback stockists from 12 August 1994.

Name:..

Address:..

....Post Code:........................

To Retailer: If you would like to stock M&B books please contact your regular book/magazine wholesaler for details.

You may be mailed with offers from other reputable companies as a result of this application. If you would rather not take advantage of these opportunities please tick box. ☐

Full of Eastern Passion...

Savour the romance of the East this summer with our two full-length compelling Romances, wrapped together in one exciting volume.

AVAILABLE FROM 29 JULY 1994 PRICED £3.99

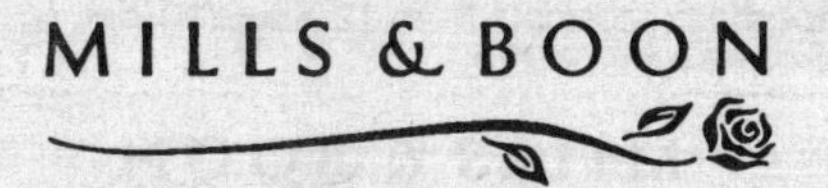

Available from WH Smith, John Menzies, Volume One, Forbuoys, Martins, Woolworths, Tesco, Asda, Safeway and other paperback stockists. Also available from Mills & Boon Reader Service, FREEPOST, PO Box 236, Croydon, Surrey CR9 9EL. (UK Postage & Packing free)

HEARTS OF FIRE

Gemma's marriage to Nathan is in tatters, but she is sure she can win him back if only she can teach him the difference between lust and love...

She knows she's asking for a miracle, but miracles can happen, can't they?

The answer is in Book 6...

MARRIAGE & MIRACLES
by Miranda Lee

The final novel in the compelling HEARTS OF FIRE saga.

Available from August 1994 Priced: £2.50

MILLS & BOON

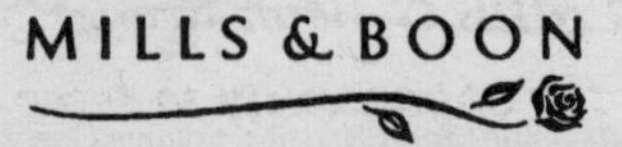

Available from WH Smith, John Menzies, Volume One, Forbuoys, Martins, Woolworths, Tesco, Asda, Safeway and other paperback stockists. Also available from Mills & Boon Reader Service, FREEPOST, PO Box 236, Croydon, Surrey CR9 9EL (UK Postage & Packing free).